# SMOKE AND MIRRORS

REED MONTGOMERY BOOK 4

LOGAN RYLES

Severn River Publishing
SevernRiverBooks.com



ISBN: 978-1-64875-539-2 (Paperback)

# ALSO BY LOGAN RYLES

**The Reed Montgomery Series**

Overwatch

Hunt to Kill

Total War

Smoke and Mirrors

Survivor

Death Cycle

Sundown

**The Prosecution Force Series**

Brink of War

First Strike

Election Day

Failed State

**To find out more about Logan Ryles and his books, visit**

**severnriverbooks.com/authors/logan-ryles**

*This one's for Jayne*

# 1

**Riga, Latvia**
**Eastern Europe**

Even as the dying glow of the sun washed Juris's face with a kiss of warmth, the autumn wind blowing off the Baltic and across the weathered Latvian coast sank through his jacket and saturated his body. Every scar and fractured bone ached and burned in the cold—constant reminders of the bloodshed over the past decade. Juris couldn't remember the first time he fell off a building and listened to his leg shatter. He couldn't recall the first bullet that ripped through his flesh or the knife that shredded his pale, European skin. Now, the scars had lost their stories and become the faceless memorabilia of every *oh-shit* moment of his life.

He stared out at the Baltic bay and watched the fishing boats churn in and out of the marinas. Unlike the scars, the boats held memories. Each battered vessel reminded him of his father's boat, not unlike these, albeit older and filthier. Juris spent the greater part of his childhood on that boat, cursing its every smelly hold and tangled fishnet. He could still hear his father shouting from the pilothouse as waves battered the creaking fiberglass hull and the wind snapped against the boom. At the time, he couldn't imagine a more disgusting and unfriendly place to spend a childhood. Now, he would give anything to go back. Anything to stop himself from boarding the nameless freighter to Albania, and the doom of a loveless, violent life that it promised him—a life where everything was counted in bodies and American dollars.

Juris stared down at the cell phone in his hand, and once again, he refreshed the email inbox, but there were still no new messages. Cedric Muri's last email came five days prior, directing him to return home to Latvia and lay low after the chaos that erupted in Atlanta. Juris was more than happy to comply. He was beyond sick of the violence he triggered every time he visited the States. In fact, he was beyond sick of everything about his sordid, criminal lifestyle. At seventeen, running from the economic wasteland of a former Soviet nation-state and falling in with a group of organized international criminals promised excitement, fortune, and a chance to make a better life for himself than what his father, grandfather, or great-grandfather had ever dreamed of.

Funny how time morphed reality, stealing away what felt most important and replacing it with the things he could never have again—things like his father, that old fishing boat, and the quiet life he led on the Baltic coast.

Once again, Juris refreshed the screen, then cursed. The downside about making a lot of money, he found, was that you never had any. For years he drowned the nagging feeling of guilt that tugged at the back of his mind with every shiny thing his blood money could buy: fancy cars, copious amounts of alcohol, loose women. Even an endangered species of cobra that he kept in his basement and fed kittens to. It all failed to wash away the emptiness his lonely life drowned him in, and in spite of a multi-six-figure income, he lived paycheck to paycheck.

But not anymore. After nearly twenty years, Juris had finally had enough. As soon as Cedric wired him his payout from the last job, he would withdraw the cash and disappear. At least for a while. Maybe he'd go to Africa and find cobras in the wild, or to Australia and watch kangaroos. The money wouldn't last forever, but it would buy him time to catch his breath and search for new ideas about how to fill the void in his soul.

Juris turned away from the balcony and walked back inside the dilapidated apartment. He crashed down on the couch, then refreshed the email browser again. Still no word from Cedric. That was unusual. Sometimes Cedric would go dark for a few days, but never this long. The Swiss broker was always good about paying his contractors on time, especially on a job as big as Atlanta.

Juris ran his hand up his arm, tracing a couple of scars that were fresher and more tender than the rest. Burn marks ran down his arm—fallout from his partner's sloppy application of gasoline to the corner of the house. The images of the dancing flames flashed through his mind, and Juris recalled the screams from inside—a woman's scream, followed by a man's. Juris stood outside and shouted for his partner, but the blond-haired Ukrainian never appeared. The flames grew hotter, singeing his face, and that was when a renegade spark ignited the traces of gasoline on his left arm. His voice joined the screams as he stumbled into a park behind the home, beating out the fire with one hand.

And still, he could hear the screams.

Juris snatched up the phone and typed a quick message to Cedric.

WHERE'S MY MONEY?

He tossed the device onto the coffee table and ran his hands over his shiny, bald head. The wind rattled against the broken screen door, filling the apartment with a clamor. Juris cursed and stomped across the room, slamming the door shut. As he did, he felt the cold edge of a knife against the back of his neck, biting straight through his collared shirt and sinking into his skin with a sting. Juris froze, his hands erupting in a new series of shudders. His gaze wandered across the room to the handgun lying on a shelf, but it was too far out of reach. He would never make it in time.

"Turn around," a voice hissed. It was raspy and broken, but he could still make out an American accent.

Juris turned slowly on his heel, sucking in another breath as the blade traced his skin and nicked his windpipe.

He could tell it was a woman by the shape of her hips and shoulders, even though she was shrouded in a thick black burka. Only her eyes—dark, brown, and full of fire—were visible through the face mask. In her right hand she clenched a long hunting knife, its razor edge glimmering in the last light of the setting sun. She flicked her wrist, and the blade cut deep into his neck, sending a surge of blood shooting out over his shoulder and onto the wall. Juris shouted, and his hands flew to the injury, desperately attempting to restrain the bleeding as the tip of the knife hovered over his face.

"*Sit*!" The word snapped with lethality, and she motioned with her free hand toward a wooden chair. Juris tried to step back, but his shoulders collided with the balcony door. The woman flicked the tip of the knife across his nose. "I said, *sit*!"

Juris stumbled backward and sat down.

The woman followed, producing a pair of handcuffs and a roll of tape from inside the folds of her burka. Her hands shook as she tossed him the handcuffs and motioned with the knife toward the back of the chair. "Cuff yourself. Behind your back."

Before Juris could object, the knife flicked toward his eye, and he jerked his head back just in time to avoid being blinded by the weapon. He closed one cuff around his left wrist before pressing both hands behind his back and fighting with the second cuff. The woman stepped behind him, and he felt the metal click into place around his right wrist. The sharp *shrick* of the tape tore through the small apartment, and Juris shuddered as he felt his hands secured to the chair, followed by his ankles. Then two thick layers closed around his mouth, muting his pleas for mercy.

The woman appeared in front of him, the tip of the knife jumping as her hand trembled. Blood dripped from its gleaming edge, staining the dirty floor beneath her feet. She reached up and pulled at the burka from behind her neck. With a quick twist of her hand, the entire garment fell from her shoulders, leaving her naked in front of him.

Juris gasped for air, his stomach convulsing at the horrific figure exposed before him. She looked like the product of a horror movie, with massive red welts covering her entire body, from her ankles to her neck. The right side of her face was a swollen mass, twisting her lips into a hideous sneer that left three of her teeth permanently exposed. Dark, dirty hair fell down over her ears, with random chunks missing from her scalp, leaving behind red, scalded flesh. Scars and burn marks spider-webbed across her chest and legs, culminating over her swollen stomach. It was as though she were a couple months pregnant, with black bruises and brutal welts massed over her navel like cancer.

Vomit rose to his mouth, but he forced it back down to keep from choking. He turned his face away, but the woman grabbed him by the chin and swiveled his head toward her. Her hands still trembled, but there was no fear or trepidation in her eyes.

"Do you speak English?" she hissed.

Tears dripped down his face as he nodded.

Her breath was hot against his cheeks. So close it stung his eyes. "Three weeks ago, you were in Atlanta. With your friend."

It didn't sound like a question, but when the blade slid into his exposed arm, he nodded admission.

"You went to a house—*my house*—and set it on fire."

Juris tried to look away. The knife sank into his arm, and he thrashed, trying to break free. The woman's viselike grip on his jaw held his head in place. He couldn't budge.

A tear slipped down her distorted cheek as she continued, but her tone remained stone cold. "You burned my fiancé alive. Destroyed my home. *You took my baby.*" She grabbed him by the left ear and jerked his face down until he was forced to stare at the mutilated mass of her stomach.

She held him, pinning him down like a bug beneath a shoe. "I killed your friend and left him in the house to burn. When the police came, they thought it was me. Guess the body was pretty much ashes by then. But I knew he wasn't alone. I heard you screaming outside. I found your footprints in the park, and then I traced you all the way back here, to this hole you call home."

Juris sobbed. His lungs heaved as he struggled to breathe through his nose, but he didn't care. He couldn't feel anything except the crushing reality of the man he had become. The knife slipped down his arm, around his ribs, and to his stomach.

"You took *everything* from me. The only happiness I've ever known." Tears rushed down her cheeks in a waterfall now, and the blade began digging into his gut. "You took my future husband. You took my future child. People you didn't know and didn't love the way I loved!"

The knife twitched and lunged into his stomach. Juris screamed, but the sound was muted by the tape.

The woman twisted the blade and dragged it across his stomach, across his belly button, ripping the entire way. She grabbed him by the throat with her free hand, pushing his head backward and growling directly into his face. "Tell the devil to keep the door open. I won't be far behind."

# 2

**Natchez Trace State Park**
**Wildersville, Tennessee**

The dying embers of charcoal in the bottom of the grill offered little warmth from the wind that whistled off the lake. Dense clouds blocked out the moonlight, but Reed knew the water was murky, swimming with God-only-knew-what manner of bacteria. Two dozen cabins lay clustered around the shore, with only a couple SUVs parked nearby. Located almost exactly halfway between Nashville and Memphis, the park was both isolated and unpopular, with no more than three cars passing the cabin each day.

It wasn't an actual safe house, but for now, it would have to suffice. Reed leaned against the deck's railing, huddled into his overcoat as he stared toward the lake. The woods that overhung the water were still, disturbed only by an occasional passing breeze. He liked it that way. It reminded him of his old cabin in the woods, back when day-to-day life was a simple pursuit of thirty kills. Before Mitchell Holiday. Before Banks Morccelli.

Reed closed his eyes and allowed the lakeside scene around him to fade from his mind. His tired body and worn focus drifted away from the burning Camaro in Nashville, the dead police officers at the Parthenon, even Banks collapsing behind the honky-tonk on Broadway. For all the chaos and carnage that had exploded around him over the past weeks, the thoughts that captured his attention now were much older—years older—dating back to his childhood. They were thoughts of David Montgomery. Thoughts of his father.

The back door of the cabin opened with a soft creak, and Banks appeared in the shadows. She wore black sweatpants and a sweatshirt, with oversized white socks and a blanket draped around her shoulders. Her cheeks were kissed with a hint of flush, but there was strength in her posture that Reed hadn't seen in days. She stepped onto the deck and settled down on the picnic table bench beside him, wrapping the blanket tighter around her shoulders.

"You shouldn't be out here," Reed said. "It's too cold."

"I've got Lyme disease. Not scarlet fever." Her tone was cynical and irritated, but not as harsh as it had been four days prior as they searched the campus of Vanderbilt University for the home of Omega Alpha Omega. Reed couldn't say there was any sympathy in her words, but at least she wasn't cursing him.

"How's Baxter?" he asked.

Reed's longtime companion, an old English bulldog, was a recent house fire survivor, with scars and singed fur to prove it. Banks fell in love with the grouchy old dog the moment she met him in Nashville and had meticulously applied his medication and cared for him ever since. Baxter hardly gave Reed a second glance these days.

"He's fine. Sleeping by the heater. Snores like a troll."

Reed didn't comment. He sat with his arms crossed and stared at the lake.

"Did you find anything?" Banks asked.

Reed's gaze drifted to the short list of names he scribbled over a legal pad littered with notes, and he ran a hand over his chin.

*Dick Carter. Aiden Phillips. Liam Holland. Mitchell Holiday. Frank Morccelli. David Montgomery.*

Over the last four days, Reed spent hours pondering those six names, to the point where he could recite them in his sleep. That list represented the members of *Omega Alpha Omega*, the fraternity and secret mythological society formed at Vanderbilt University in 1989. Of that list, two men he knew to be dead. A third might as well be. And the other three? He had no clue who they were or where to find them.

Reed leaned over the table but didn't answer Banks. Next to the legal pad was the leather-bound book of secrets for the dark fraternity. He and Banks found it in Nashville at the base of the Greek Goddess Athena statue inside the life-size replica of the Parthenon. Its pages were covered in tight rows of Ancient Greek, written by hand with an ink pen. Each symbol was perfectly crafted, consistent with every other occurrence of the same symbol. The notebook lay pinned to the table beneath six textbooks. Half the books were almanacs and translation manuals for Ancient Greek text. The others were history books detailing every known aspect of the Goddess Athena and how she was worshipped.

For a few minutes, silence hovered over the deck, then Reed realized Banks was still waiting for him to answer. He sighed and motioned to the open notebook. "Whoever wrote this wasn't using a translation manual. They *spoke* ancient Greek fluently. I've been able to translate a few things, but none of it seems to mean anything. Most of the text appears to be ritualistic prayers to Athena. The rest I can't decipher."

"Is anything in English?"

"Only the six names." Reed pulled the notebook out from under the textbooks and flipped a few pages, exposing a photograph of six men standing in front of an owl with red eyes, painted onto a grey wall. He had discovered the location where that photo was taken four days before when he and Banks broke into a frat house on Vanderbilt's campus. The owl was painted on the wall of a secret room in the attic of the home. Dried blood coated the floor, and cryptic Greek letters were carved into the wall. Next to the photograph, the list of six names was written in English. The precise handwriting matched that of the Greek text on the previous pages.

"These six names represent the members of the frat, and they appear to have titles, but I can't translate them. I don't even know who was in charge."

Banks tugged the notebook from his hands and scanned the photograph. Reed watched her gaze fixate on the tall, handsome man in the middle. He was blond, like her, with the same stunning smile. Maybe nineteen years old, with a muscular chest and the obvious vigor of an athlete. Frank Morccelli.

"Do you think my godfather was in charge?"

Reed shook his head. "Not to speak ill of the dead, but Holiday wasn't the type. He was a follower, in spite of being a politician. Based on what you've told me about your father, I don't think Frank was a ringleader, either."

Banks traced her finger across her dead father's face, then shut the book with a dull snap.

Reed lifted the half-empty water bottle off the table and took a long swallow. He stared toward the dark lake and rubbed his thumb over the crinkling water bottle wrapper. The tension that hung between them was as thick and still as the murky water of the lake, and no less cold. Reed closed his eyes and tried to imagine things were different—that things felt like they had during those fleeting moments with Banks in the cabin in North Carolina when they were snowed in and huddled next to the fire, with nothing but raging sparks between them. He recalled how it felt to touch her skin. The way her eyes sparkled when she kissed him.

How odd that something so strong and fierce could die so quickly, extinguished in an instant by the darkness and deceit of Reed's twisted life.

He *hated* himself for that.

Reed turned toward Banks and watched her huddle forward, the blanket swathed around her shoulders as she stared into the middle distance with all the emptiness of a broken woman.

"I can still see him," she whispered.

"Who?"

"The policeman. At the Parthenon." Her knuckles turned white around the edges of the blanket. "I can still hear him begging me. Begging me to help. He died right there in my arms, and I couldn't do anything to stop it."

She shook as tears slid down her cheeks. Reed leaned over the table and touched her arm.

She recoiled and glared at him. "*Why*? Why did he die?"

Reed withdrew. The iron in her glare was relentless. Demanding. He'd seen that sort of fire before. He remembered the first time he'd encountered the blazing demand for justice in a woman's stare—the woman was Private Jeanie O'Conner. O'Conner demanded justice in Iraq. Now Banks demanded justice in Tennessee. They were such vastly different women, yet the same consuming instincts of right and wrong, guilt and vindication dominated them. Concepts he was terrified to face.

"I don't know," Reed said. "I guess . . . he was in the wrong place at the wrong time. It could've been anyone."

"Sure," Banks snapped. "Could've been anyone. Anyone who stumbled into the shit show you call a life."

The words cut. Reed turned away, and Banks slapped the table.

"Look at me."

He met Banks's glare, and her teeth ground together as she leaned across the table. "This is *your* doing. Do you understand me? Men are dead because of you. My godfather is dead because of you. I'm not letting you off the hook until you make it right. Do you understand me?"

Reed nodded once but didn't speak.

She shoved the notebook toward him. "Where's *your* father?"

Reed shook his head. "It's not that simple."

"How is it not simple? Is David Montgomery your father or not?"

Reed traced the leather binding, then nodded once.

"Okay, then. Is he alive?"

Reed didn't answer.

"Look at me." The words were laden with menace, and Banks didn't blink. The resolve that filled her reminded him of the photos of Frank Morccelli inside the notebook. The apple hadn't fallen far from the tree.

Banks folded her arms again. "My father is *dead.* I'm done trading secrets with you. I'm *finished* with your lies and games. Do you hear me? I'm *finished.*"

Each word sank in and twisted like a knife in his stomach. Banks glared at him until he looked away, then she snapped her fingers. "*Look at me!* Why is your father on that list?"

Reed shook his head. "I don't know."

"Okay, then start with what you do know. From the beginning. When's the last time you saw him?"

Reed gritted his teeth. She wasn't going to back down. Every conflicted and pain-filled emotion he endured since he first saw David Montgomery's name written in that book clamored for him to refuse to talk and to hold the secrets inside. To protect himself.

But Banks was smarter than that. She always had been.

"June 4th, 1999. I was seven."

"Where?"

"Our home. Birmingham, Alabama. In the subdivisions."

Banks leaned back against the rail. "All right. What happened? Don't you dare lie to me."

Reed resumed his surveillance of the lake, rubbing his thumb into the dry pine boards of the picnic table. A splinter broke off and stabbed him in the web of his hand. He flinched and plucked it out, still avoiding her glare. "We were working on the car. Dad had this old Z/28 Camaro. '69 model. Rally Green."

"*I don't care about the car*," she growled. "Stop dodging me."

"What do you want me to say?" Reed snapped. "You want me to say he was a criminal? Fine. He was a *criminal*. The police came and arrested him right in front of me. Threw him down on the trunk of the car, read him his rights, then carted him away. I never saw him again."

"What were the charges?" There was no mercy in Banks's voice. No sympathy.

"Lots of things. Money laundering, tax fraud, securities fraud. White-collar stuff. Dad worked in finance as an asset manager and owned his own firm. He worked with wealthy businessmen."

"Where is he now?"

"Where do you think? He's in prison."

"Since 1999? The worst white-collar prisoner in the world gets out after eight or ten years. You're still lying to me."

*She's relentless.*

Reed sank his teeth into his lip until he tasted blood, then glared back at Banks. "He's not in prison for tax fraud. He's in prison for murder."

For a moment, a shadow of surprise crossed her face, but the glare returned. "Explain."

"He was serving ten years, but he was supposed to get parole after six. Something happened in prison. He snapped and lost his mind. At his parole hearing, he attacked a parole board rep and pushed her against a wall. She fell and hit her head on something—the furnace I think—and died on the spot. They charged him with second-degree murder. His lawyers pled insanity, and the charges were reduced to voluntary manslaughter, but it didn't matter." Reed stopped speaking and stared into the darkness.

"*Why?*" Banks pressed. "Why didn't it matter?"

"Because he really was insane!" Reed slammed his hand against the table. "It was like his mind just fell apart. He spoke in gibberish, forgot who my mother was . . . forgot who *I* was. They may as well have sent him to the electric chair. His brain was fried."

Reed dropped his face into his hands. His mind slipped back to that day, sixteen years before, when his mother packed their things and moved him to Los Angeles. David Montgomery's face was all over the news. The insane money launderer who murdered an innocent servant of the state. Reed's mother wouldn't allow him to attend the trial or visit him in prison. The last time he saw his father's face on anything except the news was that fateful day by the car when the police dragged David Montgomery away. Forever.

"Where is he?" Banks whispered.

"Some prison in north Alabama. Psych ward. No visitors allowed."

Banks tapped her finger against the picnic table. The soft rapping mixed with the murmur of the lake water lapping against the shore. She cleared her throat. "Your father may be the only man who knows what happened at Vanderbilt. The only man who knows who killed my father and my godfather. We need to visit him."

Reed clenched his fists. "You're not listening to me. You don't understand."

"What don't I understand, Reed? Enlighten me." Sarcasm crept into her voice.

"I called him," Reed almost shouted. A lump formed in his throat, and he forced it back. "I called him years ago after I joined the Marines. He didn't remember me . . . had no idea who I was. The man is *gone*. He won't remember Vanderbilt."

Reed crossed his arms and glared into the darkness. "There are three other names on that list, and one of them has to be alive. If you want answers, they're much better targets."

Banks raised an eyebrow. "And what if *they* are the people who killed my father? What if *they* are the men who hired you to execute Mitch?"

Reed faced her. "Then they better pray to God they have time to kill themselves before we get to them. We're not taking prisoners."

Banks pushed the notebook against his chest. "All right, then. Get to work."

# 3

**Atlanta, Georgia**

It didn't take a genius to know that every person in the room was a killer. From the brooding stares, tense backs, and cold disinterest they radiated toward one another, everything about the fifteen people sitting around the conference table hallmarked them as ruthless professionals. The arsenal of weaponry that clung to their hips, shoulders, thighs, and ankles certainly reinforced the perception.

In a word, they were exactly the sort of people Gambit was looking for. He sat at the head of the table, his hands folded on the placemat as he offered the small crowd a tight smile. Most of them didn't make eye contact —an obvious attempt to diminish his confidence and undermine his bargaining position. Gambit wasn't fooled. He'd worked in this business far too long to be intimidated by hired guns, however impressive their resumes. Of the fifteen people sitting around the table in the dim room, only one of them returned his smile. She sat at the far end of the table and leaned back with one foot on the tabletop. Her green eyes were framed by dark red hair that hung down to her shoulder blades. Unlike the others, she didn't wear a gun. Two curious-looking short swords were strapped to her outer thighs, one on each side, with the handles pointing straight up. They reminded Gambit of Japanese katanas but only half the length. *Wakizashis*, he thought they were called—some type of ancient Samurai weapon.

Even with one leg up on the table and her head rolled back, the woman had the appearance of a coiled snake. He could imagine her leaping across the room and landing on her feet in the blink of an eye, like a cobra lying in the desert sand beneath a blazing sun, only milliseconds away from delivering a death bite.

She interested Gambit. Maybe because she expressed emotion, maybe because she was the only woman in the room, or maybe because in his mind he peeled off her skintight leather jacket and exposed the iron stomach and smooth curves beneath.

Gambit was shaken from his daydream by a sly wink from the redhead. She knew, he realized. She knew what he was thinking, and she was playing him.

"If there's no money on this table in the next ten seconds, I'm gone." The man who spoke was the physical opposite of the redhead—big, bulky, and broad—in no way attractive, in spite of his muscular figure. His brown hair was scraped almost to his scalp, and his dirty fingers were held between his teeth as he bit his nails. If the woman was a sexy, coiled snake, this man was a muddy, restless bull.

Gambit expanded his smirk into a warm smile. "May I extend my sincerest condolences to you all on the loss of your employer. Oliver Enfield was a formidable man."

The nail-biter snorted. "He was a shit, and everybody knew it. What do you want, dickhead?"

Gambit rested his hands in his lap. Streaks of yellow light cut through the slits in the blinds, dancing across the conference table. The click of the big man's teeth against his fingernails broke the stillness as brashly as a church bell, grinding into Gambit's nerves and making him want to strangle the bull right in front of everyone. Nobody else sitting around the table seemed to care, but now they directed their gazes toward Gambit, waiting expectantly.

"I won't waste your time," Gambit said.

"Pretty much the only thing you've done." It was the nail-biter again.

Gambit bit back the urge to drive Nail-Biter's face against the wall and split his skull open. He wasn't afraid of any of the men who sat around this table, or the redhead at the end of it, for that matter. But there was business to attend to. Head-splitting would have to wait.

"I called you here to offer you a chance to avenge Mr. Enfield's death. As you know, he was killed by one of your own. The man they call *The Prosecutor*."

Nail-Biter snorted again. "The way I heard it, Enfield started that fight. His mistake."

Gambit sighed. "Be that as it may, the organization I represent has a vested interest in Reed Montgomery being terminated. We're prepared to offer an open contract. No stipulations. No exclusions."

A skinny man opposite Nail-Biter sat forward, his palms striking the table. "You want us to hunt one of our own? There isn't enough money in the world, you cheap—"

"What about two million dollars?"

The room fell deathly quiet, and every eye around the table snapped toward Gambit. His smile widened. "I don't take you for fools. Extend me the same courtesy. Reed Montgomery is a superior killer, and the bounty for his life has been set accordingly. The first man—or *woman*—who brings me his head will be paid on the spot, in full, in cash."

Nail-Biter sighed as if the weight of the world hung on his shoulders. "You think that's how this works? You just name a crazy number, and we go scurrying off to strangle an old friend in his sleep?"

"There are no friends in your business," Gambit replied calmly. "Least of all The Prosecutor. And I'm willing to bet that while none of you would dare discuss killing a colleague while sitting shoulder-to-shoulder, every last one of you will go to sleep tonight with his face in your dreams, his forehead in your crosshairs. And you'll be thinking to yourself, *Reed Montgomery is already dead. Somebody's going to cash in. Why shouldn't it be me?*"

The stillness that captured the room was complete. Gambit stood and rested his hands on the back of his chair. "One of you isn't as noble as the rest. One of you is acting right now, pretending to be indignant and untouchable. But tonight, that person will begin a hunt that will make them richer than fifty of Enfield's contracts, while the rest of you go to sleep with your hands down your pants like a bunch of fools. The only question is . . . who am I talking about?"

Nobody answered. Gambit monitored the body language of each killer, noting the stiffening spines and darting gazes. Gambit was no fool. He knew how these people worked. Sure, they pretended to have a code, and they wasted a lot of oxygen talking about their standards and their loyalty to one another. But at the end of the day, a killer for hire was loyal to one thing and one thing only: the payout. And the bigger that payout, the weaker that killer's loyalty to anything and everything else.

Gambit motioned toward the door. "I have the cash on hand. I'll require physical proof of Montgomery's death. Good hunting, my friends."

Every chair moved away from the table in unison, and the fifteen killers rose. Without another glance toward Gambit, they filed out of the doorway and disappeared into the hall—all of them except the redheaded woman at the end of the room. She remained seated, leaned back, one foot propped up on the table. Gambit raised one eyebrow but didn't move. Slowly, she dropped her foot onto the floor, then stood up. Every move was as smooth and effortless as a snake gliding through tall grass.

She walked around the table, flicking the fire-ember hair out of her face before tilting her head back to meet Gambit's impassive gaze. Standing only a few feet away, she appeared even smaller than he had first estimated—five-foot flat, no more. Her muscular legs were encased in fitted leather pants that highlighted every curve of her hips, right up to her waistline. The twin swords clung to her sides, strapped so tight against her legs that the handles twitched with her every breath. In spite of her stature and slender arms, Gambit had no doubt this woman knew exactly how to use those blades. A curious weapon for a modern killer, he thought. What did that say about her psyche? Did she relish the thrill of conducting her kills up close, face to face?

"Did you ever hear the story of the turtle and the snake?" The woman's voice was as soft as her lips looked. They were plump and red, coated in a thick layer of lipstick that glistened under the light cutting through the blinds.

Gambit tilted his head. "I don't know that I have."

She grinned, exposing flawless white teeth. "Well, it's not much of a story. Basically, it goes like this. A snake needs to cross a river, but he can't swim. So he asks a turtle if he can ride across the river on the turtle's back. The turtle refuses because he's afraid the snake will bite him. The snake reasons with the turtle and argues that if he were to bite the turtle, he would drown. So the turtle is convinced, and the snake crawls onto his back, and they start across the river."

Gambit slouched farther against the chair, leaning toward her as she rested one thigh on the table. Her eyes sparkled like twin emeralds, not unlike what he imagined the snake's eyes to look like in her story.

"What happened next?" he asked.

She smoothed a wrinkle in her pants and lifted her shoulders in a little shrug. "Well, when the turtle was halfway across the river, the snake sank his fangs into the turtle's neck, shooting him full of venom."

Gambit feigned shock, and she smiled. "I know, right? The turtle felt the same way. 'Now we'll both die,' the turtle said. 'Why would you do that?' The snake shrugs—however a snake does that—and says, 'I'm a snake. It's what I do.'"

The dancing fire behind her emerald gaze froze into an icy menace. Gambit straightened.

"I was just wondering," she whispered. "Are you the snake . . . or the turtle?"

She stared at him a long moment, her expression somewhere between a smirk and a sneer. Then she walked toward the door, the swords twitching on her hips with each step. Halfway across the room, she called back over her shoulder. "Take care that you don't drown yourself, my friend."

His voice was soft but laden with venom. "Who are you?"

She stopped at the door and shot him a sideways smirk. "Me? I'm Lucy. And in case you were wondering . . . I'm not a turtle."

# 4

**FBI Laboratory**
**Quantico, Virginia**

"Why are we here?" Even though Turk stood a full five inches taller than his partner, he struggled to keep up with the older man's mechanical stride.

Doors snapped back on their hinges as Agent Matthew Rollick barreled forward, flashing his FBI credentials at each checkpoint they passed.

"A burned-out Chevrolet Camaro was found west of Nashville two nights ago." Rollick's directness matched the tempo of his pounding feet. "Several witnesses placed a similar Camaro fleeing the scenes of the Vanderbilt massacre and the Centennial Park shootings."

"Centennial Park?"

"Where the Parthenon is."

"Ah." Turk scratched a quick note on a pad cluttered with scribbles, addresses, best practices, and words of wisdom from Rollick. He frowned and looked up again. "So, why are we interested in the Camaro?"

Rollick pulled his government-issue Glock handgun out of his hip holster and handed it to a guard standing at a checkpoint near two metal doors. Turk followed suit before walking through the U-shaped metal detector.

"Remember the case files you read for Atlanta?" Rollick asked. "Specifically, the shit show that went down at 191 Peachtree."

"Yeah, what about it?"

"You should remember that a black Chevrolet Camaro was spotted at that scene, also. In my mind, that makes Nashville a situation of interest."

"There wasn't a Camaro in North Carolina," Turk said.

"Nope. But there was a wrecked Land Rover. Assume for a moment that all this mess is from the same guy. Atlanta, North Carolina, Nashville. He leaves a trail of wrecked cars, doesn't he? The burned-out utility van found west of Atlanta? Or the wrecked Volkswagen Beetle just east of the Tennessee state line? Remember, the key to a successful investigation is identifying consistencies or similarities. Things that can be woven together and traced back to the perpetrator."

A buzzer rang out through the hall, followed by the metallic click of the bolt being withdrawn on the metal doors. Turk hurried to follow Rollick inside.

"What does any of this have to do with Holiday?"

"Maybe nothing," Rollick said. "Or maybe we need a bird's-eye view. Either way, it won't take but a minute to find out who owned that Camaro."

Two more hallways, then Rollick pushed through a door leading into an open laboratory. Computers lined one wall, while workbenches lined the other. Chunks of rusted, blackened metal lay strewn across the benches, each of them labeled with a yellow tag. Half a dozen forensics specialists searched through the distorted metal fragments with magnifying glasses, small metal picks, and cleaning implements.

Rollick flashed his badge at the first man and cleared his throat. "Agent Matt Rollick. I'm here about the Camaro."

The scientist wiped his hands on a towel and nodded at Rollick. "Welcome, Agent. I'm lead investigator Scully. Can I get you a beverage?"

"No, thank you. We're in a hurry. What can you tell us?"

Scully shrugged and motioned to a nearby table. Shards of sheet metal, thick steel framework, and other car parts littered the surface. Each of them was blackened by soot, except for the portions meticulously scrubbed clean by brushes and a micro pressure washer.

"Well, there's no doubt this vehicle was owned by a nefarious character," Scully said. "Most of the car was burned out before the fire department arrived. We managed to recover a portion of the vehicle identification card from the doorjamb, along with a fragment of the VIN plate from beneath the windshield. Neither one was complete, but that doesn't matter because they didn't match anyway."

Rollick frowned. "What do you mean, they didn't match?"

"We managed to piece together a full VIN number from the two cards, and we ran a search on it. The VIN is for a 1998 Toyota Corolla, even though both VIN plates match the original plates used by Chevrolet on all Camaros. Whoever owned the car deliberately manufactured fake plates."

"Terrific," Rollick muttered. "What about the engine block?"

Scully wiped his forehead with a dirty cloth. "Scrubbed. The entire VIN was ground off. Again, very deliberate."

"So, we've got nothing."

A mischievous grin darted across Scully's face. "Have some faith, Agent. They don't call me Sherlock for nothing."

Scully retrieved a closed manila folder from the counter and tapped it against his open palm. "Most manufacturers affix the VIN number to the doorjamb, to the engine block, beneath the windshield, in the glove box, and occasionally elsewhere on the body. American manufacturers also print the VIN in an undisclosed location on the frame—just for guys like me."

"Where?" Rollick demanded.

Scully laughed. "I can't tell you that. It would defeat the purpose if everybody knew. But the point is, our boy Thomas wasn't aware of it any more than you were. I was able to recover the full VIN."

"Thomas?"

"The Camaro was registered under its correct VIN to Christopher J. Thomas of Atlanta, Georgia." Scully handed the folder to Rollick.

The agent flipped it open and scanned the contents, his eyebrows rising in obvious satisfaction. He passed the folder to Turk and shook Scully's hand. "Much obliged, Scully. This is a big step."

Turk eagerly flipped the folder open and traced the front page with the tips of his fingers. Christopher J. Thomas, a middle-aged, Caucasian male. There was an address, a South Carolina driver's license number, a phone number . . . everything. Turk grinned and flipped the page, but as his gaze landed on the full-page copy of the driver's license, his smile faded like ice melting on a griddle. The photograph grabbed his stomach, twisting it until his feet felt rooted to the ground. He'd seen the face before, not that long ago. He remembered the way fireworks detonated overhead and reflected in those dark eyes.

"My God . . ." he whispered.

"What is it?" Rollick demanded.

Turk stared at the photograph a moment longer, then swallowed. "I know him. I know this guy."

Rollick snatched the folder back and frowned at the photo. "Is he on a wanted list or something? I've never heard of him."

Turk shook his head. "His name is Reed Montgomery. We served together in Iraq, but I haven't seen him since 2014 . . . when he was sentenced to death."

# 5

**Jerry Olson Field**
**Cheyenne, Wyoming**

Snow covered the flat Wyoming landscape as the plane touched down. Reed imagined he could feel every bolt rattling in the old aircraft while the wheels skipped over slight dips in the pavement, and the engines wound down. It wasn't a very big plane; the interior was outfitted with no more than forty seats, all nestled next to each other in two rows. David Montgomery used to call these sorts of regional jets "puddle jumpers." Reed remembered his father making jokes about hopping over beaver ponds on his frequent business trips around the southeast.

*What was he really doing on those trips?*

The brakes on the jet squealed as it rolled toward the terminal. Reed tapped his knuckles against his leg and stared out the window, watching airport workers dressed in orange jackets scurrying back and forth across the icy tarmac.

*God, I hope I'm right about this.*

Banks shifted in her seat and shot Reed another sideways look. The doubt radiated off of her like waves of sunlight, burning his skin and shaking his confidence.

"Why the hell are we flying all the way to Wyoming when your father is less than two hundred miles away?" That was her chief objection, and it made sense. The obvious tactic would be to confront David Montgomery in his new home, the North Alabama Penitentiary, in Winston County. Regardless of his memory gaps, it still made sense to talk to him. Ask some searching questions and gather what they could.

But Reed couldn't face David. Not now, and maybe not ever. So, he sold Banks on his wildly inconvenient plan B by reinforcing David Montgomery's insanity and arguing that David wouldn't be helpful. It was a reasonable explanation, but there was something deeper, he knew. Something more basic.

*I'm not ready to admit who David is. I'm not ready to see him as a broken, degenerate man.*

Eventually, Reed knew he would have to confront the reality of who his father had become and what his father had done—whatever that was. But for now, they needed another way to tap into the secrets behind Omega Alpha Omega, and that other way was Dick Carter, the first name on the list of fraternity members. After hours of Google searching, Carter was the only name Reed could find in the extensive Vanderbilt University Alumni files. Sure, there were articles about Morccelli and Holiday, probably due to their auspicious careers and tragic deaths, but none of the other four names bore mention in the annals of Vanderbilt class history. None except Carter.

Reed stumbled across a snapshot of a Vanderbilt yearbook that an alumnus posted publicly to Facebook. The majority of the photograph focused on his own image, of course, but in the bottom corner of one snapshot, Reed recognized Carter's distinct features—a heavy brow, round glasses, short brown hair—the same face as the young man in the cryptic fraternity photographs. Richard Hamlin Carter, a law student, as it turned out.

The photograph was for the 1991 yearbook, so Reed made the assumption that Carter was a junior at the time, which meant he was pretty heavily invested in the law program. Based on that assumption, Reed concluded that Carter probably didn't change majors before graduating, and with a field as precise as law, that meant Carter was likely still practicing.

The next step was to search for every law firm in the country that featured an associate, partner, or managing member named Dick or Richard Carter. It was a logical path to follow, but it resulted in piles of results so high Reed almost gave up. The saving grace of the endeavor were the attorney headshots most law firms featured on their "About Us" page, and after three solid hours of sifting through hundreds of websites, Reed found a face that only a mother could love: a heavy brow, round glasses, and brown hair.

Dick Carter, Attorney at Law. Lusk, Wyoming.

That discovery led to a plane ride from Memphis to Dallas, Dallas to Denver, and then Denver to Cheyenne. They could have flown directly to Wyoming if they returned to Nashville first, but Reed was more than a little concerned about the heat that awaited them in Music City.

"You better be right about this," Banks muttered as they piled out of the puddle jumper and into the tiny Wyoming airport.

"Nobody hopes that more than me," Reed said.

"Why couldn't we just call him?"

"Because if he is who we think he is, he doesn't want to be found, and he doesn't want to talk. Fifteen hundred people live in Lusk. The closest big city is Casper, with thirty thousand people, and it's over an hour away. He's not practicing law. He's hiding."

Reed dropped the fake South Carolina driver's license on the counter of the rental car dealership and offered a brief nod to the sleepy-eyed clerk.

The young man smiled and tapped on a keyboard. "Do you have a preference, sir?"

"Four-wheel drive. Looks yucky outside."

The clerk laughed. "Welcome to Wyoming."

Reed loaded their single duffle bag into the back of the Dodge Durango that waited outside and wrapped his jacket tighter around his numb body. The sky was a murky grey, boiling with clouds that swept in from the west over the plains. Snowflakes drifted down onto the prairie and melted against the warm engines of the planes idling nearby. He imagined Cheyenne must be a beautiful place during the summer. Right now, it was too cold and hostile.

The SUV hummed as the tires hit the asphalt. Lusk lay over two hours north of Cheyenne, assuming they could maintain highway speeds. With the snow piling up next to the pavement and the temperature still dropping, Reed wasn't about to get in a hurry.

Banks sat huddled in the passenger seat, tracing the freezing glass of her window as she stared out over the prairie. Her breath misted against the glass, and she drew irregular shapes in the fog with a delicate index finger. "What happened to the car?"

Reed frowned. "What car?"

"The Camaro your dad owned. What happened to it?"

Reed kicked the wipers on to fight the swirling snow and relaxed off the accelerator a little more. "Why do you ask?"

She shrugged. "Why not?"

*A fair answer.*

Reed leaned back into the seat. It was wide and comfortable, but his shoulder blades still ached.

"Part of my father's original sentence included fines. He couldn't afford to pay them out of pocket, not even close. So, the state seized his private property . . . including the car."

Banks pushed the hair out of her face, still looking through the glass. She folded her arms, and for a while, the hum of the tires dominated the small cabin. "Can I see it?"

"See what?"

"The picture of the car."

"What makes you think I have a picture?"

Banks turned toward him and rolled her eyes. "When I asked about your father, the first thing you mentioned was the car. You knew the year, the model, the color. I know you have a picture."

Reed sank his fingernails into the leather-wrapped steering wheel and pretended to ignore her. She narrowed her eyes at him. Reed sighed and dug his hand into his pocket. His worn wallet fell open, and he slid the faded photograph out of the rear compartment. Banks cradled it in her open palms as though it were a newborn kitten.

Reed glanced into the side-view mirror, avoiding the photograph. He didn't need to look at it to remember every detail of the tattered and faded image. The green Camaro sat by a lake, and his family settled on the grass with their backs leaned up against the fender. David Montgomery sat with one arm around his wife and his free hand resting on his six-year-old son's shoulder. Sunlight glinted off the Z/28 logo next to David's arm. It was a perfect moment. Or at least the closest thing Reed could remember to a perfect moment.

Banks handed the photograph back. Without a word, Reed tucked it into the back of the wallet and crammed it into his pocket.

"When did you last see your mother?" Her tone was surprisingly soft. The venomous edge that tainted her every word since he found her in the Nashville bar a few days prior receded, if only for a moment.

Reed wiped his nose with the back of his hand. "I don't know. Five, six years ago."

"She still in Los Angeles?"

"Yeah, I guess."

"You should go see her."

"Is that right?" he snapped. "When's the last time you saw *your* mother?"

Banks glared out the window. Reed felt an immediate twinge in his stomach, and he swallowed back the bitterness that swelled inside of him like a tidal wave.

"I'm sorry," he muttered. "That wasn't fair."

Banks's face twisted into an ugly glare. "You know something, Reed? I don't know why I ever gave a crap about you. You're a twisted, nasty person, and as soon as we find out who killed my father and I've had my way with them, I'm done with you. Do you hear me? *I'm done.*"

Every word ripped through Reed like a bullet. He watched the white lines running down the road ahead of him and tried to forget that Banks was there or that any of his family ever existed.

*I'm here to avenge Kelly. Then I'm more done with myself than Banks could ever be.*

# 6

**State Capitol Building**
**Baton Rouge, Louisiana**

"You should have told me the *moment* he contacted you!" Dan's voice boomed through the executive office, filled to the brim with frustration and fear.

Maggie reclined in the leather chair, keeping her hands rested on the arms. The office was cold, too cold for comfort, but it helped her stay awake. She hadn't enjoyed a full night's rest in days. Not since her men were gunned down in the family cabin outside of Lake Maurepas. As governor of Louisiana, her days were often overwhelming and exhausting, but this past week had taken everything up a notch. Well, more than a notch.

Her lieutenant governor pounded back and forth across her office, his expensive leather-soled shoes clacking against the hardwood. The bald man wearing round glasses and sitting in a wingback chair in front of Maggie's desk watched Dan stomp around. He shot Maggie a sideways questioning look as if to say, "*Are you going to tolerate this?*"

"Dan, I think you should sit down," Maggie said.

Dan snapped his fingers and turned his gaze toward the ceiling. "Sit down? Oh, is *that* what we need?"

"Dan." Maggie snapped with sudden command. "Sit down. Right now."

Dan's back stiffened, and his hand fell to his side. His cheeks flushed a little, and he hurried to the second chair in front of Maggie's desk. He shifted on the cold leather and cleared his throat. "I'm sorry, Madam Governor. That was inappropriate. It's just that—"

"We're all stressed, Dan."

Dan nodded but didn't reply, choosing instead to stare out the window, over the skyline of Baton Rouge. Maggie indulged him, watching his shoulders sag. He was just as exhausted as she was and probably hadn't slept in days—the impact of his ferocious dedication.

Maggie placed her hands on the desk and met the bald man's gaze. He raised his eyebrows, and she held up one finger before he could comment. Robert Coulier was the newest addition to her cabinet, the emergency replacement for the attorney general who was assassinated two weeks prior in his own home. A special election would be held later that year to officially fill the AG's office, but for now, Robert Coulier was the man for the job. Maggie called him her pit bull, and for a good reason. He was ruthless and relentless. She tried not to overthink the fact that he only took the job to advance his own ambitions of revenge against some local business adversaries.

Maggie turned back to Dan. "Look. You're right. I should have told you when Gambit reached out to me for a meeting. At the time, I thought it best to confront him on my own."

"Gambit?" Dan said. "Is that what he called himself?"

"That's the only name he would give me."

"And you believe him? You believe this man killed Attorney General Matthews?"

Maggie shrugged. "He never said so directly. In his invitation to a meeting, he only referenced 'responsible parties.' I think the implication was clear."

Dan raised his hands toward the ceiling. "He was *right there.* In Baton Rouge! Maggie, we could've arrested him!"

Maggie coughed with unnecessary force.

Dan shrank back and rubbed his hand over his forehead. "What I mean is, I think it was a missed opportunity."

"It wasn't an opportunity," Maggie said. "What were we going to arrest him for? Emailing me? Lots of people do that."

"He knew who killed Matthews," Dan insisted.

"He *implied*. Nothing more."

"You said he tried to bribe you. Blackmail you, even. That's illegal."

"True. And I could've arrested him for it, but where would that leave us? A blackmail charge is a few years in jail, at most, and puts us no closer to cutting the head off the snake."

"He *threatened* your family!"

Coulier sat forward, clearing his throat. "Mr. Lieutenant Governor, I think perhaps you should have more faith in your boss's ability to manage this situation."

Dan shot Coulier a murderous glare. "I'll get to you in a minute!"

Maggie slammed her hand against the desk. "Dan, that's enough. You will not address the attorney general or myself in this fashion any further. Do you understand me?"

Dan continued glowering at Coulier a moment longer, then straightened the wrinkles out of his pants with a great deal more production than was necessary.

Maggie waited until the silence became awkward, then took a sip of water. "When I received the nomination, what did you say, Dan? Do you remember?"

Dan nodded. "Of course I remember. I told you I believed in you. That I wanted to see you win because you were different. You could make a change."

"That's right. And the change we need is a spring cleaning like Louisiana has never seen before. We knew there was corruption in this state, and not just in the government, but in the corporations, businesses, industries. Everywhere. And we believed the good people who live here shouldn't endure the waste, prejudice, and universal harm that corruption burdens them with. Am I right or wrong?"

"Of course, of course. You know I believe that."

"When you rattle chains, dogs start snapping at you. We knew this would happen. The way I see it, it's a good sign. It means we're on the right track."

Dan rubbed his face. "I just don't like the idea of you exposing yourself like that. We need you. The whole state needs you."

"I agree. And I admit I could have been more cautious. It's something to improve on in the future, but for now, we need to run this lead to ground. Mr. Attorney General, what are your thoughts?"

Coulier adjusted his glasses and scratched his chin, then nodded as if he were agreeing with himself about some unspoken problem. "The first thing to do is to apply pressure, Madam Governor. We need to know exactly who our adversaries are. The quickest way to identify them will be to make them nervous. If they know we mean business, they'll strike back hard, and that could expose them."

Maggie tilted her head to one side, pondering each word. "Okay. What do you propose?"

"It's difficult to determine where to hit them if we don't know what they're up to. We know this *Gambit* approached you for the purpose of soliciting your participation in whatever it is he's doing. We can conclude that Attorney General Matthews was assassinated because he threatened this same operation. I think you need to put yourself in their shoes for a minute. If you were running an illicit operation out of Louisiana, and you needed the help of the governor, what sort of thing might you be up to? Try to remember. What did he ask you for?"

Maggie looked past the two men, her gaze fixated on the bookcase behind them. Her mind drifted back to the restaurant in Baton Rouge, where she met the man who referred to himself only as Gambit. She searched her memory, recalling every word, every gesture, and the way his expressions changed as he spoke.

She faced Coulier. "The port. They're operating out of New Orleans. He mentioned wanting help with getting permits approved. Unless they're in construction, which is something I wouldn't know a lot about, he must be talking about shipping. If they're involved in international shipping, the governor's office could be a valuable ally."

Coulier nodded. "Or a ruthless enemy. So, you know where their weak spot is. Close the port."

Dan sat up with all the energy and severity of a lightning bolt. "You can't *do that!*"

Coulier sighed and slid his glasses off, wiping the lenses with a cloth from his pocket. "The port is run by private industry, yes, but it's still regulated by the state. There is precedence to close the port by executive order in times of emergency. It was closed during Hurricane Katrina, for example."

Dan ran both hands through his thinning hair. "That was during a legitimate crisis. Thousands of lives were at stake! If you close the port in order to pressure an invisible criminal entity who *might* be using it for illicit activity, trust me, articles of impeachment will hit the House floor within the month. Hundreds of people will be out of work. The state will lose *millions* of dollars. It's the seventh-largest port in the *nation*, for God's sake!" Dan stared at Maggie with wide, pleading eyes.

She took another sip of water, then redirected her attention to Coulier. "He's right," she said. "That's a big risk. I'm not concerned about being reelected, but if I'm impeached in my first year, there's not a lot of good that I can do for the state."

"Big risks for big rewards, Madam Governor." Coulier returned his glasses to his nose. "Something an old mentor of mine used to say when I was a kid fresh out of law school: *go for the throat*. If you want to make the pig squeal, you might have to spill some blood."

"Spoken like a man who *wasn't* elected and doesn't answer to anyone," Dan said.

"He answers to me." Maggie's tone carried a sudden edge, and Dan froze. "As do *you*, Mr. Lieutenant Governor." She turned toward Coulier. "Having said that, I can't simply close the port on a whim. I need a reason, and that reason can't be flushing out corruption. Executive orders require some level of emergency."

A slow smile drifted across Coulier's lips. "Well, Madam Governor, it's a good thing you've got a pit bull on hand who knows how to sniff out an emergency."

# 7

**FBI Laboratory**
**Quantico, Virginia**

"Walk me through it again, Turk. One step at a time."

Agent Rollick sat at a small table in the laboratory cafeteria, poking at a mound of dry potatoes with his fork. Turk stared at his own plate, and for a moment, his mind was swept away from the DC facility, thousands of miles across the ocean to the brutal desert of Iraq. He remembered sitting in a mess hall across from Montgomery, poking at potatoes that were every bit as dry and bland as these. He could still taste the sweat on his lips. Feel the grind of damp sand between his thighs with every step. Hear the blast of gunfire from the streets of Karbala as their fire team fought to reach Baghdad.

It was years ago, yet it only felt like days.

"He was my corporal in Iraq," Turk said. Each word took effort, searing its way through his throat as he spoke. "He directed our fire team. Him, me, and a guy from Idaho named Johnson. We ran reconnaissance missions in the desert. Usual stuff for Force Recon."

"When's the last time you saw him?" Rollick spoke through a mouthful of peas.

"November of 2014. At his trial."

"He was court-martialed?"

"Yeah . . ." Turk trailed off as he stared at the South Carolina driver's license printed with Christopher J. Thomas as the owner. The face had aged, acquiring additional lines, while the eyes were harder and colder than he recalled. But there was no doubt in his mind. The man in the photograph was definitely Reed Montgomery.

Rollick snapped his fingers inches away from Turk's nose. "Hey, I need details. What was he on trial for?"

Turk blinked, then cleared his throat. "Murder. Five counts."

"Five counts? Holy shit. In Iraq?"

"Yeah. There was this private . . . O'Conner, I think her name was. She was our driver on an escort mission. We were moving two tankers of diesel into Baghdad and came under fire. Johnson got hit pretty bad. A couple other Marines died. Anyway, there were these contractors on the job—mercenaries. Their Humvee went down, and they refused to leave it. After we got to Baghdad, O'Conner discovered that these guys were smuggling artifacts out of Iraq. That's why they wouldn't abandon the Humvee. She told Montgomery, and apparently, he was going to do something, but I didn't know anything about it at the time. I ran into him later that night. He was carrying his rifle, headed toward the contractors' motor pool. I stopped him, but he wouldn't talk. He killed all five of them."

Rollick's eyebrows shot up. "For smuggling?"

Turk shook his head. "No. According to Montgomery, the contractors found out that O'Conner was gonna bust them, so they raped and killed her. He found her body, then he shot them."

"Was that corroborated?"

"Yeah. All the evidence was there. DNA from three of the contractors was found on her body. Boot prints put at least five people at the scene. They also discovered evidence of smuggling. Dozens of artifacts were hidden in the Humvee."

"But Montgomery was still court-martialed."

"Of course." Turk ground his thumb into his napkin, smearing off dried bits of cranberry sauce. It was days like this, stuck miles from home in some dreary cafeteria eating imitation food, that he wanted nothing more than to be broke and happy back in East Tennessee. Where life was simple. Where your best friend wasn't a killer. "I mean, he murdered five people. Sure, they were scumbags, but he still killed them."

"You said you saw him at the trial?"

"Yeah. I was a key witness for the prosecution. Turns out, I was the last person to see him before he shot those guys."

"So you saw him headed their way with a gun and didn't report it. Why weren't you charged with accessory to murder?"

Turk didn't look up. The question should have put him on edge, but there was no aggression in Rollick's question. Only curiosity.

"There was nothing to report. I saw him walking across camp with a rifle. He was a Marine—a spec ops Marine, at that. Nothing he was doing was unusual."

Rollick grunted and took a sip of instant coffee. He swished it in his mouth, then set the cup down. "What was the ruling?"

"Guilty, of course. I mean, the evidence was overwhelming. He pleaded not guilty, but in his closing statement before the sentencing, he admitted to all five counts. He just didn't think it was wrong."

"What was the sentence?"

Turk swallowed down a gulp of unsweet tea, then wiped his mouth with the napkin. "Death. They sentenced him to death."

Rollick pushed his plate away and tugged the paper closer to him, studying the photocopy of the driver's license. He ran a finger behind his lip to pry out a piece of dry turkey, then scratched his chin.

"He's not a bad man," Turk said. "I fought beside him for two years. Would've given my life for him. He would've done the same for me in a heartbeat. That's why he did what he did. Because they hurt one of his own."

Rollick laid the paper down. "You need to get something straight, kid. We're not here to judge people or excuse them. That's a jury's job. We're here to gather evidence and catch the bad guys. I don't really care if this guy is Santa Clause. As things stand, he's linked to some pretty brutal shootings in Nashville, and probably more carnage back in North Carolina and Atlanta. Don't confuse the man you fought beside with whoever this guy has become. People change."

Turk nodded but didn't meet Rollick's gaze. He stared down at his plate and tried to push away his last memory of Montgomery, but it was too clear in his head. He could hear the gavel ringing out in the courtroom. He could see the guards dragging his friend toward the door and the resignation in Montgomery's stare as he mouthed a final farewell toward Turk.

"It's crazy. It felt like losing a brother when they took him away."

Rollick wasn't listening. He had his phone out and remained fixated on the screen. Turk rubbed his forehead and tried to make sense of the mess that was evolving in front of him. None of it added up. Nothing made sense.

"There has to be a mix-up," Turk said. "Montgomery's in prison."

"I wouldn't be so sure of that." Rollick handed Turk the phone. The screen was illuminated with an email, and PDF scans of official documents lined the bottom half of the message.

"What am I looking at?" Turk asked.

"After you identified the driver's license photo, I had a file pulled on Corporal Reed Montgomery. Everything Uncle Sam had on him."

"And?"

"After the ruling, he was housed in Colorado's Rock Hollow Penitentiary. Apparently, Leavenworth was undergoing renovations at the time, so they loaned him out to a state facility."

Turk flipped through the paperwork. Each file detailed a different part of Montgomery's sad story: photos of the dead contractors, images from the trial, and records from his sentencing and discharge. Nothing that surprised him. "And then?"

Rollick cleared his throat. "And then nothing. He disappeared. No records, no documented escape attempt. No discharge or appeals court or anything. One moment he was a prisoner in Colorado, and the next, he never existed."

# 8

**Lusk, Wyoming**

Reed's initial intuition was correct. Dick Carter wasn't practicing a lot of law in Wyoming. The little town reminded him of the tiny Alabama towns his family drove through while cruising in the old Camaro, albeit a lot windier. An American flag flapped at the top of a pole staked in front of the post office. The streets were wide and empty, with only a few cars passing every few minutes. Snow piled up against the sides of brick buildings, accentuating the murk of the sky.

Carter's private law firm was sandwiched between a sub shop and a hair salon, right in the core of downtown. The windows were smudged with dirt, reminding Reed of the old cowboy movies with downtowns lined by brick buildings with muddy windows.

*This guy attends a premier university in a big city, then goes to work all the way out here? No way.*

Reed kicked the snow off his boots on the front stoop of the office, then waited for Banks to clamber out of the Durango. Her face flushed in the blast of wind, but she pulled herself up onto the sidewalk without a second glance at the snow-swept town.

"I've got a lot of bad memories of you and me in the snow," she muttered.

"That's funny," Reed said. "I've got a lot of good ones."

Banks rolled her eyes and pushed past him into the office. A bell rang overhead as the door creaked open, and Reed tasted the dull, sooty odor of a kerosene heater. The warmth that flushed his skin was refreshing, though, and brought relaxation to his taut muscles.

"Good morning." A bright, cheery voice spoke from the other side of the receptionist's desk. The woman was middle-aged, maybe late thirties, with thick lipstick and curly blonde hair that was obviously dyed. Her blouse clung to her skin with all the form-fitting aggression of a synthetic bodysuit, the neckline diving deep over her chest and exposing excessive amounts of cleavage.

*Well, he's certainly made himself comfortable in exile, hasn't he?*

The door clapped shut on a spring, and the woman smiled. "Can I help you?"

"We're here to see Mr. Carter." Reed spoke abruptly and instantly regretted it.

The woman recoiled a little, her smile fading. "Do you have an appointment?"

"Mr. Fletcher referred us," Banks broke in, offering the receptionist a warm smile. "We're looking to get divorced."

Reed shot Banks a sideways look.

Her momentary glare chilled him to the bone before she turned the smile back toward the receptionist. "A quick divorce," she added.

"Oh, I see. Mr. Fletcher, of course." She nodded at Banks, her gaze turning icy as it passed Reed.

*Great. Why am I always the bad guy?*

Skinny fingers adorned with acrylic nails clicked against the receiver as the woman lifted it to her ear and punched the intercom button. "Dick? Yes, I've got a young couple here to see you. They said a 'Mr. Fletcher' referred them. Yes? I'm not sure. It's about a divorce . . . Right. Okay."

She hung up, then motioned them toward a door behind her desk. "He's only got a minute, but he can see you now."

Banks led the way, shoving in front of Reed and smiling again at the receptionist.

*Oh, you're working this one, aren't you? Trying to win the divorce you're not even having.*

Reed resisted a smirk that tugged at the corners of his mouth. Somehow, someway, this ferocious side of Banks was every bit as intoxicating as the sweet side. Knowing there was a brutal edge beneath her flashy demeanor didn't alarm him. If anything, it ignited a fresh curiosity in his tired soul.

*I don't have time for this. I promised her we're here for vengeance, not reconciliation.*

The office was small and musty. Thick volumes wrapped in muted colors packed one bank of shelves, while an impressive collection of ships-in-bottles were stacked along another, meticulously crafted but layered with dust. An executive desk in the middle of the room overflowed with piles of paperwork and more books stacked next to a laptop computer. The man sitting behind it resembled the picture of the frat kid perfectly, as though almost nothing had changed: a heavy brow, round glasses, and brown hair. Only now, grey peppered the brown, and the forehead was more wrinkled than that of the college freshman. This man had seen things. Endured things. The secrets he housed had worn away at his soul for decades.

Carter stepped around the desk, offering a tired smile as he extended his hand. A brown blazer swished against an oversized cotton shirt that hadn't been ironed since it was new. He didn't wear a tie, and tangled brown chest hair poked its way through an unbuttoned collar.

"Dick Carter," he said. "A pleasure to meet you."

Banks shook his hand, and he turned to Reed.

"Chris Thomas," Reed said. "Thank you for meeting us on such short notice."

"Can I get you any refreshments?" It was the receptionist.

Reed shook his head, and she ducked out of the room, closing the door behind her. Banks helped herself to one of the leather-wrapped chairs in front of the desk, and Reed joined her, dusting off the chair with one hand before sitting. Everything was dirty.

Carter sat down and pushed his glasses up. "I only have a few minutes, but Shelly said you needed to discuss a divorce? I'm afraid I don't know a Mr. Fletcher. Perhaps you had me confused with another attorney."

"No, you're the attorney we're looking for," Reed said. "And I'm pretty sure you don't have any appointments this afternoon. By the look of it, you rarely have any appointments."

Carter frowned. "I'm sorry. How can I help exactly?"

Reed glanced at Banks, tilting his head to one side. She shrugged as if giving him permission to be himself. Letting him off the leash.

*May as well cut to the chase.*

"We're here about Mitch Holiday."

The color drained from Carter's face as though his blood was being sucked out of his body with a vacuum cleaner. He shook his head and started to stand. "I'm afraid I can't help you. Shelly will show you out—"

"Please sit." Reed leaned forward and grabbed Carter by the sleeve, propelling him back into the chair with a quick twist of his arm.

Carter landed in a cloud of dust, and Reed could feel the tremor in his arm as he blinked back a stream of sweat running off his forehead.

Banks looked pale again but spoke with all the iron of a flawlessly healthy woman. "My name is Banks Morccelli—Frank Morccelli's daughter. You knew my father, didn't you?"

Carter shook his head and held up both hands. "No, no, no. I'm not talking about any of that. Now, please leave before I call—"

As Carter reached for the phone, Reed snatched the trailing end of the cord from the side of the desk and jerked it out of the wall.

"Mr. Carter, we're not here to hurt you. But you're going to need to work with us. Trust me when I tell you that I'm the least of your concerns."

Carter's look of fear—the panic, mixed with a desperate desire for self-preservation—was an all-consuming terror Reed had seen before, in the woods outside of Atlanta as he interrogated Senator Mitchell Holiday.

"I'm not talking," Carter spluttered. "I've got nothing to say."

Banks leaned across the table, reducing the space between her and the frightened lawyer to only a couple feet. "Mr. Carter, my daddy died in New Orleans. They say it was a drunk driver, but I think you know the truth. His closest friend and my godfather, Mitchell Holiday, was murdered by a shadowy organization that he identified as *'from end to end.'* We believe that had something to do with the fraternity you shared at Vanderbilt. Omega—"

"Don't say it!" Carter almost shouted the words as his body tensed.

The door crept open, and Shelly appeared, her face twisted into a frown.

"Dick? Everything okay?"

"It's fine." He waved her away, wiping sweat from his forehead with his free hand. "Go turn down the heat. It's sweltering in here."

"Dick, it's barely seventy degrees."

"Shelly!" Carter slapped the desk.

The receptionist jumped, then disappeared back into the lobby, the door smacking shut behind her.

Carter ran the sleeve of his jacket across his face, then glared at Banks. "You said Mitch was killed. How do you know? The police are still investigating."

"We know because I was the one hired to kill him," Reed said. His voice was flat and toneless, but Carter reacted nonetheless, starting to stand again.

"*Relax*," Reed snapped. "I'm not here for you, and I didn't kill Holiday. Somebody else did, and they're dead now if it makes you feel any better."

Carter's face twisted between Banks and Reed. He lifted a bottle of water off the desk and drained it. "What do you want?"

"We need to know about the fraternity," Banks said. "We found the book. We know about the cult. We also know that three of the six original members are either dead or otherwise removed from the picture."

"You mean David Montgomery," Carter said.

"Yes. We know David is in prison, suffering from mental illness."

Carter snorted and stared at the wall, grinding his thumb into the leather arm of his chair.

"What?" Reed demanded.

"David isn't mentally ill," Carter muttered. "At least not naturally so."

"What are you saying?"

Carter shook his head and continued to rub his thumb deep into the leather.

Reed smacked his hand against the desk. "Hey! This is important. David is my father. You understand me?"

Carter frowned. "Wait . . . you're David's kid? I remember he had a boy."

"That's right. I'm his boy. I know he was convicted of money laundering, then of manslaughter. You said his mental illness wasn't natural? Explain yourself."

Carter looked away again. "I'm sorry. Your father was . . . a brilliant man."

"What happened to him? I need to know."

Carter shook his head again, harder this time. "No. If I tell you, I'm as good as dead. You shouldn't be here!"

Once again, Carter started to stand.

Reed beat him to it, leaning over the desk and shoving him into the chair. "*Listen to me.* My father is mindless. *Her* father is dead. Mitch Holiday is dead. I don't want your name on that list, but if you don't tell me what I need to know, nothing can save you. Do you hear me? They'll come for you. It wasn't that hard to find you."

Carter rubbed both palms against his pant legs as sweat dripped from his nose.

*Dear God, this man sweats like a pig.*

"Do you think I'm hiding, boy? They've left me alone because I didn't talk. If I talk—"

"Mr. Carter . . ." Banks walked around the desk and took one of his hands in hers. She rubbed her delicate thumbs across the back of his hand and stared up at him with unabashed pleading. "My father was everything to me. He was my world. Somebody stole him away. Somebody stole my godfather away. They stole Reed's father and one of his dearest friends. The bloodshed isn't stopping here. I don't blame you for being afraid. But if you don't help us, nobody will. I know you're a good man. That's why you got out and came all the way up here. Be a good man now. Do the right thing."

Carter stared down at her, and Reed saw something cold and hard crumble behind his gaze.

He squeezed her hand. "You're Frank's girl?" he whispered.

Banks nodded as a tear slipped down her cheek.

Reed stepped back from the desk, lowering his hand and waiting, giving the moment to Banks.

"I knew him," Carter said. "Frank was . . . a good man. Maybe the only one of us who wasn't crazy from the start."

Banks smiled. "That's my daddy."

"You look like him," Carter said. "You have his eyes. His kindness."

Banks squeezed his hand and waited.

Carter's shoulders slumped. "Okay, I'll tell you. For Frank."

# 9

**Lusk, Wyoming**

Carter settled back into the old desk chair. It creaked with as much drama as an eighty-year-old man. He ran his hand over his face and sighed. “Chris, or whatever your name is, there’s a bottle of bourbon on the shelf over there. Do you mind?”

Reed stepped across the room and poured a tall glass of liquor from an unmarked bottle. Carter gulped down a few swallows, then set the glass on the desk.

“Mitch was always a bourbon guy. Hell, Mitch would drink anything. He settled down a lot, the last I talked to him.”

“When was that?” Banks asked.

Carter forced a weary smile. “When you were born.”

“You were there?” Her shock was evident.

Carter shook his head. “Oh, no. I haven’t left Wyoming in almost thirty years.”

“That much divorce work going on up here?” Reed asked.

Carter snorted. “Don’t patronize me, boy. I’m still your elder, even if you think you’re tougher than me.”

“Fair enough. Why, then?”

Carter swirled the drink. "I wasn't like the others. Everybody else had a family or a girlfriend. I was an orphan and got into Vanderbilt on a scholarship. So, when things got ugly, I guess I had no reason to stay. I came up here, finished school at UW, set up shop. Been paying bills ever since."

"What went ugly?" Reed asked. "What happened?"

Carter swallowed repeatedly as if the bourbon was burning holes in his throat. "You said you found the book?"

Reed nodded.

"In the Parthenon, right?"

"Yeah."

Carter laughed. "I figured as much. Liam was obsessed with that place. He's the one who kept the book. In fact, he's the one who started the whole thing."

"What thing?" Banks pressed.

"The fraternity. The entire dark, nasty business . . ."

Carter trailed off again, and Reed exchanged a glance with Banks. He could see the hesitancy in her posture, but they couldn't afford this continued ambiguity.

"So, Liam founded the fraternity?" Reed asked.

"Liam was . . . special. It wouldn't surprise me if he had some manner of obsessive-compulsive disorder. Like I mentioned, he was absolutely infatuated with the Parthenon. He attended Vanderbilt, exclusively, so he could be close to the monument. To him, it wasn't just a museum; it was an actual holy place. A goddess-ordained recreation of the original Greek temple."

Reed didn't know what to say. He just lifted his eyebrows.

"I know," Carter said. "Sounds crazy, doesn't it? It was crazy for us, too. But you have to understand, the rest of us weren't like Liam. He grew up someplace in New England. A real liberal, wild home. He yearned for structure and authority. I guess, for him, it felt like security or belonging. But for the others, well, they were all from conservative Southern homes. I was an orphan, as I mentioned, but foster homes are much the same in the South. Strict and traditional. So for us, we didn't really get the whole infatuation with Athena or any of the mysticism. But we loved the rebellion of it all, you know? Like I said, we all grew up really conservative. Everything about Liam's secret organization felt forbidden and mysterious, so we bought in and founded it with him. For me and Mitch, Frank and Dave, I think it was just an adventure. Something to do."

"But not for Liam," Banks prodded.

"No. Liam went hardcore. I'm not exactly sure where he sourced all his theology and practices from, but it wasn't exclusively Ancient Greek mythology. There was a lot of dark paganism mixed in. Stuff from Africa, Asia, the Caribbean. Liam spent hours poring over holy books from a dozen religions and spoke a lot about a 'deeper truth' and 'hidden power.' Typical cult stuff. The rituals were the most disturbing."

"You mean the sacrifices," Reed said. "The rabbits."

Carter grunted. "You must've seen the pictures."

"Yes, and the blood on the floor in the attic."

"The rabbits were a Saxon thing—some connection with Easter and ancient pagan practices. I'm not entirely sure. Liam would buy them at a pet store and then dismember them as part of our . . . worship, I guess. It was altogether horrific. By the time we realized what we were mixed up in, it was too late."

"Too late for what?" Banks asked. "Why couldn't you just leave?"

Carter rubbed his knee. "Aiden."

"Aiden?" Reed said. "You mean Aiden Phillips? The sixth member of your fraternity?"

Carter nodded. "Aiden was . . . Well, Aiden was really something. He was two years younger than any of us—seventeen when he enrolled in Vanderbilt. Dave and Frank were brilliant, but Aiden . . . Aiden was a genius in the truest sense of the term. He saw the world differently than those around him, not in terms of reality or relationships, but in terms of opportunities and risks. Everything was a calculated decision for him. He didn't understand the concept of a consequence as anything other than a payment. If you cheat on a test, being caught and failing a class could be a consequence, a price. But it wasn't a moral thing for him—just a mathematical penalty—like the price of a gallon of gas. An objective consideration."

"You're telling us he was a psychopath," Reed said.

"People throw that word around a lot these days. But in some ways, yes, he was. He didn't maintain any deep relationships with anyone, but people found him charming. Seductive, even. Liam was particularly enthralled by him. Aiden supported Liam's research and pagan practices completely, supplying him with anything he needed. Liam's obsessive-compulsive traits quickly bonded him to Aiden in what can only be described as an intimate way. Don't get me wrong. It wasn't sexual. But in every other fashion, they were soulmates. Partners."

"What happened? Why didn't you leave?" Banks said.

Carter placed his face in his hands. "I'm devastated by what happened to Mitch and Frank, and just as devastated by what happened to Dave, but nothing I tell you will change any of it. Do you understand me?"

He lowered his hands and stared at each of them in turn. In the minutes that passed since they first stepped into the office, Carter looked like he had aged a decade. His hair stuck up in disarray, and his cheeks sagged. The burden of secrets so long-kept ground him down faster than the years ever could.

"You need to tell us," Reed said. "This isn't stopping unless it's *stopped*."

Carter made a dry, humorless sound. "Piss and vinegar. I like you, Chris. You've got your dad in you."

"My dad," Reed said. "David Montgomery. He went to prison for money laundering and financial crimes. Did that have something to do with the fraternity?"

"No, it had something to do with what came after. With what Aiden did."

"I need to know." Reed's voice became hard, with just a tinge of desperation. He leaned close to the desk and stared Carter down.

The old lawyer reclined in his seat. "Nothing I tell you will bring any peace. It's a rabbit hole, Chris. A Pandora's box. Trust me when I say you don't want to open it."

"You're right. I don't. But I have to. This isn't just about my dad or hers. It's about all the people who have died because of whatever secret you're keeping. Tell me. What happened to my father?"

"He went insane," Carter stated bluntly. "He lost his mind."

"I'm aware of that. With no history of mental illness in my family, he cracked—"

"It wasn't genetic."

"Come again?"

"Your father's insanity wasn't instigated by bad genes or a brutal prison life. He knew things, Chris. He knew a lot more than I know, just like Frank did. Just like Mitch did. The difference is you can't frame a drunk driver in prison or hire an assassin and write it off as political."

"What are you telling me?" Reed said.

"I'm telling you it's a lot harder to kill a man in a white-collar penitentiary than it is to slip him a few drugs and turn his brain into mental mush. When secrets are at stake, and the person pulling strings has no conscience, anything is an option."

Reed sat back in the chair. A weight descended into his stomach, and his head began to spin.

*That's not possible.*

Carter placed both hands on the table. His gaze, while still full of fear, turned hard and cold. "What Liam and Aiden started has grown into something much darker and much larger than a rabbit-killing fraternity hidden in the attic of an old house. If you want to know what happened to your fathers, the truth—"

A sudden buzzing blasted from the desk. Banks jerked upright, and Carter's gaze snapped toward the intercom. Before he could hit the answer button, the door blew back on its hinges. Reed didn't bother to look over his shoulder. He already knew what stood behind them. Diving to the left, he wrapped his arms around Banks's shoulders, toppling them both to the floor as the first gunshot rang out. Carter screamed, and then the second gunshot split the air.

Reed kicked his chair out from under his feet and rolled to the left. Shelly stood in the doorway, a revolver clamped between her shaking hands as she pivoted the barrel toward them. Her eyes were alive with fear and desperation, and her hair exploded into a cloud of static around her scalp. The gun cracked again, and this time the bullet slammed home into the hardwood floor inches from Reed's arm. He rolled over again, toppling across Banks before he reached the shelf. The rows of ships-in-bottles lined the bottom shelf, and Reed wrapped his fingers around the nearest one, flinging it toward Shelly with all the force he could muster while lying on his side. The bottle spun through midair like a knife, then shattered directly over her forehead. The gun dropped to the floor, and Shelly followed it, blood draining over her face.

Reed scrambled to his feet and pulled Banks up behind him. He stopped next to Shelly, who was lying on the floor, shrieking in pain. He couldn't see the extent of her injuries between the mess of blood and her clawing fingers, but he could tell she couldn't see him.

Reed scooped up the revolver and cocked the hammer.

Banks caught him by the arm and jerked the gun away from Shelly's writhing body. "No! She's suffered enough. There's no need to kill her."

Reed lowered the gun and looked down at the woman. He caught sight of the pain in her face, distorted by blood and tears. He didn't see the hatred of a monster or the ruthlessness of a killer. Only the broken, shattered soul of a woman who was backed into a corner and forced to do things she never dreamed herself capable of.

Reed nodded to Banks and glanced back at Carter. The lawyer lay on the floor, one bullet wound in his stomach, and another in his chest. There could be no doubt he was dead the moment the second shot tore through his heart.

"Come on," Reed said. "They're coming."

# 10

**Tampa, Florida**

Everything tasted of salt: the wind, the sand that stuck between Lucy's lips, the sweat that dripped off her forehead and drained into her mouth. She inhaled a deep breath of hot, humid air and relished in the relaxation that built in her chest then dissipated down her limbs. Her fingers ached with the strain of supporting her full weight, but somehow, even the stress relaxed her. This was stillness. Emptiness. Peace.

There wasn't really a word to describe the place her mind faded into when she joined body and soul and expelled both physical and mental pollutants. Suspended here on the rail of her penthouse balcony, overlooking Tampa Bay as the sun descended toward the water, her soul found rest in an invisible harbor. Each practiced yoga pose drew her farther out of the prison of the physical realm and deeper into a more honest reality—a reality where she perceived herself as she truly was, identifying individual emotions with perfect clarity, not for the sake of self-enlightenment so much as self-liberation.

Lucy balanced on the edge of the balcony with both hands pressed between her legs, her open palms riding the smooth surface of the polished rail. Her legs were spread apart, sticking out over the precipice, suspended four hundred feet above the harbor. The height didn't bother her, and neither did the breeze that encapsulated her tan body and challenged her balance. She leaned back, offsetting the weight of her legs by the extension of her head back over the balcony. Muscles rippled beneath the bare skin of her stomach, gleaming with sweat but unstrained. Red hair fell down from her scalp and traced the floor of the balcony, and Lucy exhaled a slow, satisfying sigh.

With a gentle flex of her hips, she twisted on her palms, lifting her shoulders until they skimmed across the top of the rail, leaving her hair dangling over the precipice. She settled her thighs against the rail, hooked her feet around the spindles of the balcony, then let go.

The moment her body fell backward, into hundreds of feet of emptiness, was always her favorite. With her eyes closed, she bent at the knees and allowed her arms to fall outward on either side until she dangled outside the balcony, hooked by her bent legs. The wind snapped against her hair and flooded her lungs, but she didn't feel stress. No fear tainted the otherworldly thrill of dangling from the top of the penthouse tower. It was perfect, total acceptance, a mood so pure and untouchable that she really wouldn't have cared if the railing collapsed, and she fell to her death.

It would've been worth it.

Lucy opened her curled fingers and relished the kiss of the sun on her skin. The railing dug into her calves, but her mind drifted away from the realities of the temporal world, and she embraced a state of spiritual revelation. It was at this point she found her clarity and solved her most troubling problems.

She exhaled through her nose as she forced the remnants of clutter out of her mind and asked herself the same question she always asked at this moment: *What do I see?*

Gambit. Her mind drifted back to the meeting in the boardroom in Atlanta. The other killers circled around the table. Lucy knew them all by call sign, if not personally: *Zeus*, the former spec ops soldier from Greece; *Cowboy*, the wild, reckless assassin from Oklahoma; *Secretariat*, the free-spirited strangler with a penchant for rural kills.

Oliver gave all his people call signs and preferred that they address each other exclusively by those names. To Lucy he bestowed the handle *Little*

*Bitch*, a derogatory commentary on both her stature and gender, hastily crafted to demean her. Lucy loved the name and quickly developed it into her own brand—the only female killer on Oliver's payroll. A woman who used neither guns nor explosives but would poison or decapitate a victim in a heartbeat. Lucy didn't like to think of herself as a violent woman. She preferred the imagery of an ancient Japanese warrior—specifically the mythical female type. Noble. Ruthless. Brutally effective.

*What do I see?*

The question repeated itself as the sunshine radiated off her skin, and she dove deeper into her memories. She saw another face she knew well: dark hair, a heavy brow line, a deep, penetrating stare. She knew this man —*The Prosecutor.*

*Why do they want him dead?*

Lucy wondered what Reed Montgomery had done to garner the wrath of Oliver Enfield. She never trusted Oliver and doubted that Reed did either, but the old English killer wasn't in the habit of slaughtering his greatest assets, his killers. Reed was respected as one of the most ruthless and effective assassins in the entire company. Rumor had it that he was also one of Oliver's indentured killers, a man who traded a predefined number of contracts in exchange for some expensive favor from Oliver. Lucy wasn't aware of the details of Reed's arrangement, but it didn't matter. Most of Oliver's killers were indentured. In fact, Lucy was one of the few who worked for the old man by choice, and really, she didn't even work for him. She worked *with* him, on occasion, when his resources served her own goals. Oliver had never backstabbed or undermined her, although she had little doubt he was capable of both. What had The Prosecutor done to push the old man over the edge?

Lucy felt her brow wrinkling with concentration, and she forced herself away from the enticing arms of intensity and back into the folds of relaxation and openness.

*Reed.*

She knew his face and what a relentless fighter he could be. She had only met him twice, but neither occasion was the type of encounter a person easily forgot. As her mind dissolved into mental oblivion, she saw the flames again, licking up the sides of the building, trapping her at every turn. There was literal blood on her hands, dripping from the edge of her short sword as she fought her way through smoke-filled rooms and searched for a doorway. A body lay behind her—the body of a Chinese mob boss. She decapitated him and left his corpse in the bathtub, but not before the fire broke out in the restaurant below, consuming the old Manhattan building in mere seconds.

Lucy didn't know that another killer lay on his stomach across the street, staring through the scope of a sniper rifle. She didn't know that he watched her enter the building, approach her prey, and draw the sword. Reed had come to New York for the same reason as she did: to kill Li Chung. But unlike Lucy, Reed wasn't there for vengeance. He was there because Oliver Enfield paid him to do a job. After Lucy dropped her blade on the back of Chung's neck, Reed could have packed up his rifle, taken credit for the kill, and left. Lucy would've burned alive, the victim of the fire she lit to cover her tracks.

Lucy opened her eyes and stared out over Tampa Bay, upside down. She let her arms hang loose as she envisioned the big man bursting through the door, holding a cloth over his face. Lucy was almost unconscious as Reed scooped her up and kicked his way through the back door. A moment later, she lay in the back of his getaway car, gasping for clean air as The Prosecutor whisked her away from New York, away from the fire, and away from her victim.

*"I don't know who the hell you are, but you suck at arson."*

That was the only thing Reed ever said about the incident. An hour later, he deposited her at a hotel, dropped a roll of twenties on the nightstand, and walked out. Lucy tried to get his name, tried to make him stay, but The Prosecutor was gone as quickly as he came, vanishing into the murky underworld he lived in.

She might never have seen him again if her personal crusade against evil hadn't led her to Oliver Enfield's doorstep. Lucy lived with one primary goal, one thing that pulled her out of bed every morning: destroying bullies. She hated bullies with every part of her soul, but vigilante ass-kicking was expensive work. Oliver offered her the chance to perpetuate her crusade *and* be paid for it.

And that was when she met Reed for the second time. Just once, in passing, walking out of Oliver's downtown Atlanta penthouse at the same moment Lucy was walking in. Reed met her gaze for a split second, barely long enough for recognition to flash across his face. Then he winked once, without the hint of a smile, and slipped through the doorway.

Lucy ran one hand through her long, flowing hair. With a quick twist of her hips, she picked herself up, swung over the rail, and landed on the balcony. Her head spun for a brief moment, but her body felt light and free. All the stress and anxiety of her daily life had faded, and she found focus and clarity again.

Stepping through the sliding glass door, back into her living room, she lifted her sword belt off the coffee table and slipped one blade out of its sheath, admiring the glimmer of fading sunlight on the razor-sharp edge, then slammed it home again with a flick of her wrist.

She wasn't sure what Reed had done to back himself into this corner. She didn't know who Gambit was or why he wanted The Prosecutor on ice. None of that really mattered. The only thing that *did* matter was that Reed Montgomery wasn't like the others. He wasn't a killer by choice, but by predicament. Montgomery was a good man, and she owed him her life.

If they were going to kill The Prosecutor, they were going to have to kill Little Bitch first.

# 11

**J. Edgar Hoover Building**
**Washington, DC**

"Turk! Let's go. They found Montgomery."

Turk stumbled to his feet and crashed out of the cubicle.

Rollick thundered past with a single sheet of paper clamped in one hand, then shoved the page into Turk's fingers and headed for the door.

Turk rushed after him, fumbling with the page as he stumbled into the elevator. He opened his mouth, but Rollick held up a finger as he lifted his phone to one ear.

"Yes, Gwen? This is Rollick. I'm headed to the airport right now with my partner. We need a jet fueled and ready to fly, ASAP. We're headed to Wyoming."

Rollick hung up, then adjusted his tie and looked at Turk. The big former Marine stared down at the page and the single photograph it contained—a grainy security-camera image of a tall man with broad shoulders moving through the TSA line at a regional airport.

"Well?" Rollick asked.

Turk nodded once, then lowered the photograph.

"Your boy, Montgomery, was flagged by TSA only moments after he left

Cheyenne Regional Airport in a rental car. We had his alias, Christopher J. Thomas, listed as a person of interest, but the fool running the checkpoint didn't see the flag until Montgomery was already gone."

"Where is he now?" Turk asked.

Rollick raised one empty hand toward the ceiling, then started toward the parking lot. "No idea. It's a big state, but there aren't many interesting places to go. Unless he's running, my guess is he'll return to the airport pretty soon. We'll work on contingency plans during the flight."

Turk hurried to follow Rollick to the nearest jet-black Tahoe. Ronald Reagan Washington National Airport was only ten minutes away, but Turk had a feeling Rollick would make it in five.

The engine rumbled, and Turk glanced back down at the page. The image, while grainy, was clear enough to make out the strong jawline and defined features of the man directly in its center. There was no denying the hard brow line and stern glare. Textbook Reed Montgomery.

"I need to know something before you get on my plane," Rollick said suddenly.

Turk looked up. "Yeah?"

"If it comes down to it, could you shoot this guy?"

Turk hesitated. He remembered the last time he saw Reed's face, twisted in defeat as they wheeled the former Marine away to prison. Away to his death. He was a good man. A man Turk thought he knew and trusted. And in the end, that good man had become an unreserved killer. Rollick had said people changed, but maybe Reed never had. Maybe Turk's old rifle buddy had always been a killer, and now, he was off the leash.

Turk folded the paper and dropped it on the dash. Without looking at Rollick, he nodded once. "Yeah, if I had to."

Rollick grunted. It was a noncommittal sound. "All right, then. Let's hope you don't have to."

# 12

**HWY 18 West, Wyoming**

"I . . . I don't get it." Banks's voice wavered, and Reed thought she was passing out again.

A quick glance at the passenger seat dissuaded his fears. Banks sat upright, staring at her hands that were stained with Carter's blood. Her fingers didn't shake, but confusion clouded her face.

"I don't either," he said. "It's a lot weirder and darker than I imagined." Reed flipped the heater off. In spite of the bitter cold outside, the cabin of the Durango felt thick and stuffy.

"So, my dad was . . . a cultist?" Her brow furrowed over pale cheeks.

"I don't think so. The drift I got from Carter was that Liam was the cultist. Everybody else was just swept along for the ride."

"Everyone except Aiden."

"Yes. Except Aiden."

"Do you have any idea who that is?"

"I couldn't find anything on Liam or Aiden when I was searching last night. Carter was the only person I could dig up."

"Do you think they're still alive?"

"At least one of them is." As soon as the words left his mouth, the reality sank in.

"So, whoever is alive," she said, "they're the one killing everybody. They're the one who killed my dad."

"Looks that way. They must've been the one to order the Holiday hit, also."

"And poison your father?"

A knot twisted deep inside Reed's stomach. His hands twisted around the wheel of the car, and he heard Carter's words again, as strong and as clear as they had been less than thirty minutes before.

*"When secrets are at stake, and the person pulling strings has no conscience, anything is an option."*

So, that was it. David Montgomery hadn't gone insane in prison. He was poisoned and intentionally transformed into a blabbering vegetable.

"It's Aiden."

Banks looked up. "What?"

Reed clenched his fist. "Aiden is the one behind this. Remember what Carter said? He said, 'When the person pulling strings has no conscience, anything is possible.' Aiden didn't think of things in terms of right or wrong or good and bad. He was completely amoral. A textbook psychopath."

"So, Aiden killed my father?" She struggled to blink away a tear.

Reed felt a sudden tug at his heart. It was that same familiar ache he felt when he looked too long into Banks's deep blue eyes. The ache of a man who longed to hold her, sweep her off her feet, and wipe away the burning pain that consumed her. Cautiously, he reached out and touched her arm.

Banks looked up, and her face turned to stone. "I want you to find him," she hissed. "You want to make things right with me? You find this man, you find out what he did, and you punish him for it."

Reed met her gaze, facing the hatred he saw. It hurt him. The anger and malice in her heart blocked out the beautiful, innocent soul he first met. The soul he fell in love with at the top of that parking garage in Atlanta.

"I promise," he said. "Whatever it takes."

Banks held his gaze a moment, then turned away and clenched her fists around the loose ends of her sleeves.

Reed watched the snowfall and fought the urge to grab her hand. More than anything, he wanted to jerk the car to the side of the road, pull her close, and kiss her so long and soft. Hold her and promise her that no matter what, come hell or high water or years of war with these faceless enemies, *he* would be her hero. He would shield her from the bullets, take the heat himself, and give his life to give her the peace and resolution she demanded. No price was too great. No battle too costly. This woman was his soul. Being near to her, even if she hated him, was the closest thing to being home Reed had ever known.

*I want her back. So help me God, I want this woman back.*

"Once you do that," Banks said. "Once you find this man and punish him, I want you gone." Her iron rage ignited into a bonfire, but this time, that blaze was directed at him. "I want you to take yourself and your lies and all your wretched, disgusting hurtfulness, and leave."

Every word cut through Reed like the blast from a shotgun. Sweat pooled between his fingers and the steering wheel, and it was all he could do to push back the tears that begged to break free. "Banks, I—"

"I don't want your excuses. I want you to do your job. Make this right. And then I never, ever want to see you again."

---

The miles that hummed under the tires were the only sound to break the silence as they drove back to Cheyenne. Banks stared out the window the entire time, her arms crossed and her features blank. Reed tilted his head away from her until his vision began to clear, and he regained control of himself. Snow continued to flutter down outside the car, building in the crevice between the side-view mirror and the doorjamb. Even as the wind whistled beneath the bumper and the sky turned from grey to black, the coldness of impending winter couldn't match the icy claws of defeat that sank into his heart.

*No matter what I do or how hard I fight, I will never overcome the monster I am to her.*

A street sign flashed by next to the highway, advertising the airport ten miles ahead. Reed twisted in his seat and swallowed back the self-loathing. There would be a time to hate himself, and a time to mourn the lost love and the wretched tragedy of it all, but not now, not today. Right now, he had to get Banks out of Cheyenne.

"We'll get a plane to Memphis and find some food. Once we get back, I'll find Aiden."

Banks didn't acknowledge his comment, but he knew she was awake. He cleared his throat and wiped his sweaty palms against his pants. "You have a mother in Tupelo, right? I think—"

"I'm not going home." Her words were cold and sharp, with a tone of finality.

"I understand you have issues with her," Reed said. "If you like, I can set you up an apartment someplace safe and—"

"You misunderstand me. I'm not leaving *you* until the job is done. I want to meet the man who killed my father."

Reed turned off the highway, following the signs into the airport. Nightfall, mixed with the swirling snow, blocked his view of the terminal, and he slowed as the road curved. "I don't think that's a good idea. Trust me, Banks. This isn't a path you want to lead yourself down."

Banks snorted. "You think I'm going to let you waltz off with the promise of hunting this man down? I'm not letting you out of my sight until you deliver. Worry about your own damnation, and I'll worry about mine."

Reed slowed to a stop at a traffic light and tapped his finger against the steering wheel. "Okay, let me put it another way. *You'll get in my way*. I don't think you're prepared for what it'll take to—"

"Where will you start?"

Reed hesitated, but he already knew the answer. There was only one answer. "My father."

"You're going to visit him?"

"They don't allow visitors."

"I guess you'll have to break him out, then."

"Banks, I can't just—"

"Whatever it takes. Isn't that what you said?" Banks turned an icy glare on him.

Reed looked away and ran his tongue over dry lips, then he nodded slowly. "Yes. Whatever it takes."

"Good."

Reed steered the SUV toward the rental car drop-off. "Are you hungry?"

Banks grunted. "I could eat."

"I think there's a Burger King inside the airport. You find some food and . . ." His voice drifted off as he stared over the dashboard. In the distance, through the swirl of snow, two men approached the SUV. Both wore black jackets and black pants and stepped out with the confidence of trained professionals. Through the corner of his eye, Reed noted a jet-black Tahoe parked twenty yards to his left. Glancing into his rearview mirror, back toward the guard shack that barricaded the entrance of the airport, Reed saw that the gate was now lowered. The man inside the booth stood at the door, one hand resting on his gun. Reed depressed the brake, sliding to a stop on the snow-covered asphalt. He thought he saw the two men quicken their step.

"What is it?" Banks asked.

"These guys . . . they're not—"

Through the swirling snow, the lead man stepped toward the Durango. He was tall, with broad shoulders, and had the commanding stance of a man used to barging into places where he wasn't welcome. Each stride was practiced and powerful, but he lifted his feet a little too quickly, as though he were used to wearing boots, not shoes. His big hands shoved the blazer back, and Reed saw him place his fingers around the grip of a handgun.

The snow drifted apart, and for the first time, Reed saw his broad features and keen eyes. Even though the sky was obscured by clouds, Reed imagined he could see fireworks casting alternating pools of blue and red light across the man's weathered cheeks.

*No way.*

# 13

Turk could barely discern the outlines of two people sitting behind the foggy glass of the SUV. The Durango still ran, with exhaust fumes gathering under the rear bumper. Dim running lights glinted against his face, and he took another two steps forward, pushing his jacket open and placing one hand on his pistol.

"Steady, Turk," Rollick warned. "Don't spook him!"

The blend of sleet and snow was blown away by a sudden gust of wind, exposing a clearer view of the driver. Their gazes met in an instant, and Turk felt himself jerked away from the cold and the wind, and back to Iraq.

Reed sat behind the steering wheel, leaning forward and squinting toward the men who blocked his path. Turk stood frozen, the gun hovering just below eyeline. Reed glared a challenge at him, and Rollick barked from behind.

"Identify, Turk! Is that him?"

Turk wanted to respond. He felt the confirmation building in his mind, but it was trapped behind his throat. He felt immobilized as the sudden reality of the identity of the man sitting behind the wheel struck home.

Reed's inquisitive squint faded into a glare, and Turk watched his hand slide toward the shifter.

"Don't do it, Reed," Turk whispered.

But he knew that look. The look of determination and blind obsession. The same unstoppable and relentless look he saw in Reed's eyes in the moments before Corporal Montgomery gunned down those five civilian contractors in Iraq.

Turk told the jury the same thing he told Rollick—that he saw Montgomery walking across camp with a rifle. But that wasn't true, or at least, it wasn't the whole truth. Turk confronted Reed that night. Stopped him at the barracks, saw the look in his eye, and knew then what he never admitted to anyone—that Reed was on a mission for blood. Whatever Reed was about to do, neither the powers of Heaven nor the forces of Hell would stand in his way.

Turk jerked the gun from his belt and raised it to eye level, screaming across the parking lot. "*FBI!* Get out of the car!"

# 14

**Cheyenne, Wyoming**

Reed met Turk's gaze, and again he could taste the dry, dusty air of Iraq. As his mind traveled back, all those years ago, the memories of the fireworks and the band playing "The Star-Spangled Banner" were as clear as if they happened yesterday. He could see Turk standing in front of him, his shoulders squared and steady. Turk, his fellow Marine, and maybe his only friend. A man who had his back in Iraq, saved his life more than once, and stuck to his side like a tick on a hound. A man that had, on that fateful night, tried to stop him.

He could still hear Turk's last words, echoing over the fireworks: *"Don't do it, Reed."*

Turk's eyes, blurred through the falling snow, were saying the same thing now. *Don't do it. For God's sake, don't do it.*

Reed set his jaw and slid his hand down the wheel, placing it against the shifter.

Turk snatched the concealed Glock from his waistband holster and screamed, *"FBI! Get out of the car!"*

Reed shoved the SUV into reverse and planted his foot into the accelerator, sliding the Durango backward in a screech of rubber and asphalt. The second agent stepped forward to Turk's left and drew his gun.

Reed shoved his hand against Banks's shoulder and shouted over the roar of the motor. "Get down!"

The dull pops of handgun fire were barely audible above the wind, but the sound of shattering glass rang as clear as a bell. The rear bumper of the Durango collided with a parked pickup, and the vehicle came to a crunching halt. Reed kept his head beneath the dash as he shoved the SUV into gear, then spun the wheel to the right.

"Stay down!" he snapped, but it wasn't necessary.

Banks leaned close to the floorboard, doubled over with both hands over her head.

Reed guessed the direction of the entrance gate and mashed the gas. The tires spun against what now sounded like dirt, and Reed risked a look over the dash just in time to miss a metal guardrail next to the ditch. The Durango hopped back onto the pavement, leaving the shouting FBI agents in its wake as Reed plowed toward the guard shack by the entrance. The flimsy gate snapped in half over the front bumper of the Durango as the security guard huddled inside his shack.

Reed sat up and blinked against the wind that blasted through a series of holes in the windshield. Fragments of glass lay scattered over the dash—the victims of the five or six bullets that found their way into the cabin. In spite of the spiderweb cracks, Reed could make out the road ahead with enough clarity to swerve past oncoming cars. The airport wasn't all that busy at this time of day, but the snowfall made it difficult to see more than twenty yards ahead. The windshield wipers skipped and snagged against the cracked glass, further inhibiting his view.

"Were they really FBI?" Banks's question was spoken in measured, toneless calm.

Reed couldn't tell if she was angry, terrified, or embracing some form of self-inflicted insensitivity. "I think so. Here for me."

Reed jerked around another sedan, then glanced in the rearview mirror. A black Tahoe roared toward him, closing the distance between them like a race car fighting for first place.

"They're back," he snapped. "Hand me the revolver."

Banks tossed the handgun into the glove box and slammed it shut. "No. These aren't the bad guys. They're just doing their job."

A snapping sound rang out from behind them, and the back glass of the Durango cracked.

Reed ducked. "Yeah? Well, they're *shooting at me*!"

Reed pushed the Durango harder, squinting at a green sign pointing left toward Fort Collins, Colorado. He wasn't sure how far away the state line was, but it wouldn't matter. Turk would radio Colorado Highway Patrol and have them waiting for him long before he could lose the Tahoe. State police would block off the entire freeway if they needed to. Taking the interstate would be a deathtrap.

*Unless . . .*

"Open the GPS!" Reed swerved just in time to miss a pothole.

Bank's delicate fingers skipped over the large screen as she opened the SUV's built-in navigation system. "What am I looking for?"

"Water! Any kind of bridge. Preferably on the highway."

She zoomed in on their current location, scanning through the map before jabbing her finger at an irregular blue circle. "There! The interstate crosses some kind of small lake. What are you doing?"

"Betting on that Tahoe being two-wheel drive." Reed pulled the wheel to the left, swerving into the turn lane just in time to take the ramp onto I-25 South. In the rearview mirror, he saw the Tahoe skid and then careen toward him, following him up the ramp and onto the freeway.

"How far is the bridge?"

Banks shook her head. "I can't tell. Maybe half a mile. What are you doing?"

"Hold on to something. This is gonna be hairy."

"No, no. I don't like hairy!"

Reed double-checked the selector switch, ensuring the Durango was still in four-wheel drive, then pressed the pedal to the floor. He watched the blue outline of the lake draw closer on the dash, highlighted by the backlit screen as the speedometer passed seventy miles an hour. He watched the Tahoe falling slowly behind, and a moment later, the pursuing vehicle vanished altogether just as a yellow sign loomed up on the side of the road.

WARNING: BRIDGE MAY ICE IN COLD WEATHER.

Reed slammed on the brakes, and all four wheels of the SUV locked up, screaming against the pavement. The bridge was only yards ahead as the Durango careened forward. The black asphalt of the roadway vanished, giving way to the smooth concrete surface of the bridge as Reed released the brake and rested his foot on the gas. The SUV continued to slide, the back end fishtailing as Banks let out a little shriek.

"Reed! The edge!"

Reed counter-steered and applied just a hint of gas, expertly breaking the slide before bringing the SUV to a halt right in the middle of the ice-covered bridge. He glanced into the rearview mirror and saw the hulk of the Tahoe break through the fog, hurtling down the highway and plowing straight toward his bumper.

*Wait for it.*

"Hold on," he hissed, and Banks dove beneath the dash again, covering her head.

The nose of the Tahoe dove toward the pavement as the driver identified the stopped Durango only yards ahead and slammed on the brakes.

*Too little, too late.*

The Tahoe's bumper crossed onto the bridge only a moment later, and the locked front wheels of the big SUV broke traction instantly, sending the back end spinning around onto the concrete as the driver completely lost control.

Reed smacked his foot against the gas, grinding the wheels against the bridge and sending them shooting forward only a split second before the spinning Tahoe swung toward them. The Durango skidded ahead just as the Tahoe's rear bumper completed a full swing, smashing into the smaller SUV's taillight before screeching toward the guardrail at the side of the bridge.

The four-wheel grip of the Durango saved them. For a moment, as Reed felt the girth of the Tahoe spinning behind them, he thought it would make a direct hit and send them both rocketing into the icy water below. Instead, the Durango grabbed the concrete beneath the thin layer of ice, and an instant later, they were shooting toward the asphalt again. Just as they crossed off the bridge and back onto the highway, a bone-jarring crash ripped through the air. In the foggy side-view mirror, Reed saw the Tahoe blast through the flimsy guardrail. It hopped the edge of the bridge and fell toward the dark grey water below.

Unaware that he had held his breath for the last thirty seconds, he let out a sigh and slouched into the seat. The momentary, instinctual gratification of survival flooded his mind—a prehistoric instinct more powerful than any guilt or regret.

He looked into the mirror again, but he couldn't see the bridge. It was gone, swallowed into the gathering storm.

"Oh my god," Banks whispered. She sat rigid, her focus fixed on the side-view mirror. "Did you kill them?"

Reed swallowed past a dry throat. "No, they'll make it out."

She ran shaking fingers over her face. "Oh my god," she whispered again. "What have you done?"

Reed wiped his nose across the back of his hand and cleared his throat. "Banks, look at me."

Her shoulders trembled now.

"*Banks*, look at me." His tone sharpened, and Banks met his gaze. "You're alive," he said. "Sometimes, that's the only thing that matters."

"They were cops. *Good men*, Reed!"

"Probably. And right now, they're probably more pissed than they've ever been, but you can't dwell on that. If you want to catch the bastard who killed your father, things like this happen. Do you understand me?"

Banks rubbed her palms against her kneecaps and nodded.

"Good," Reed said. "We're going to Alabama."

# 15

**John F. Kennedy International Airport**
**New York, New York**

The buzz of several thousand voices filled the terminal, echoing off the walls and creating a constant clatter of shouts, objections, and the exhausted complaints of jet-lagged travelers. Kelly had worried that once she left the Islamic-saturated security of southeastern Europe, the black burka she wore would become more of a beacon than a disguise—especially in a New York airport.

She needn't have worried. The airport was full of travelers of every ethnicity—Hindus, Indonesians, Australians, Africans, South Americans. She wasn't the only woman wearing heavy Muslim garb, either, although she was probably the only white woman in that demographic. Even so, with only the top of her nose and her brown eyes visible between the folds of her head-to-toe clothing, she was much less visibly white than most of the few hundred women packed in around her.

Bottom line, she wasn't hiding anything in the folds of her hot and heavy wardrobe. At least, she wasn't hiding a weapon. The brutal scars that crisscrossed her body from the ankles up were more horrifying to look at than any bomb or handgun. They contorted her skin, discoloring it into a tapestry of blacks, blues, and reds. Dry and dying skin hung in tags all over her torso, and each step or sweep of her arms ignited blinding pain.

But she didn't scream. She didn't cry. Not now. For days after the two-story Canton home came crashing down around her, she cried. Sitting naked on the floor of half a dozen hotel rooms, she rocked back and forth as her hands cradled her disfigured stomach, and tears flowed over her brutalized face like a waterfall of grief. The physical agony that racked her body, however excruciating it was, couldn't match the mental and emotional chaos that ruled her soul. She couldn't sleep or eat, and she could barely stand. When she slept, haunted images of her fiancé burning alive on the floor, trapped beneath a fallen roof beam, consumed her mind. She recalled herself fighting through the smoke, coughing and screaming as she struggled to free him. She remembered the way her lungs felt ready to explode—filled to capacity with toxic fumes. And then, the sudden lurching pain in her abdomen. The first wrenching contractions of a trauma-induced miscarriage.

Those ravaging memories tore through her brain in a constant, never-ending montage of visions and echoing screams since she crawled out of the ashes, leaving the burning body of one arsonist in the smoke behind her. For hours after the fire, as she lay in a muddy ditch a hundred yards from the house, she wasn't sure if she was alive or not. The visions, hallucinations, and dominating pain were so vague, so confusing, that she thought she must be slipping free of the physical constraints of reality and falling straight into the bowels of Hell.

But no, she hadn't died. In the cruelest twist of fate, her body survived —scalded from head to toe and horrifically disfigured, but not fatally harmed. The smoke must have caused the hallucinations, and the trauma certainly bore the blame for her inability to claw her way out of the ditch and seek the help of the paramedics that swarmed her home. By the time her mind returned to a state of semi-consciousness, those paramedics were long gone, leaving the smoldering ashes surrounded by yellow police tape —standard procedure for a fatal house fire with an undetermined cause.

Kelly wasn't sure why she didn't trust the police. Maybe it was her career as a luxury car thief—years spent evading anyone in uniform to the point where, when her mind grew weary, and her focus faded, she reverted back to what she knew best: hiding. Or maybe she simply didn't believe that the men and women in blue were capable of serving the type of justice her soul craved. For whatever reason, when Kelly awoke in the hospital the next day, she didn't wait to find out what had happened or who had rescued her. She tore the IVs from her arm, swiped a bottle of painkillers, and before they could stop her, slipped through the door, vanishing back into the confused tangle of Atlanta suburbs.

It took days to put herself back together. Her bank accounts were restricted, pending closure after the processing of her estate. Everybody thought she was dead, and she had no desire to contradict them. Her family was already consumed by the throes of wrenching grief—a feeling she now knew more intimately than she ever thought possible. Sure, she may not be dead now, but she would be very soon. There was no point in exposing her survival only to force her aging parents to experience the devastation of loss all over again.

Instead, she kept her identity a secret, using cash and fake IDs she had stashed in the back of a local library—relics from her past that she shouldn't have kept. She bought the burka, treated her wounds, and kept herself alive.

Then she flew to Europe. Only one thought kept her lungs filtering air through her body: the commanding, instinctual, burning desire for blood. First, the blood of the man she saw fleeing her home, leaving his burning companion behind, and then the blood of the man she had once loved more dearly than she loved herself. The man who held her, kissed her softly and made love to her to the serenading rhythm of the sea washing against the sand under French moonlight. The man she trusted and believed in, even when she shouldn't have. The man who betrayed her, took her fiancé, her baby—her whole world. She thirsted for the blood of Reed Montgomery.

Kelly sat huddled next to the airport's wall, a chill rippling across her fragile skin in spite of the thick garment. Her hands shook, even as they were clutched close to her sides, but it wasn't because of the chill. Her hands always shook now, the nerves permanently savaged by the bite of the flames.

The sting of fresh tears ran down her face, and she swallowed the emotion back, burying her feelings inside an invisible vault that had replaced her soul long ago. She shut the door and turned the key. The thick walls of the vault, built of resentment, bitterness, and fear, allowed only one emotion to radiate through them: anger. Burning, raging anger. The sort of flame that was fueled by a blend of malice, crushing grief, and rage all at once. A confused, roaring mess of fire.

It was that feeling that pulled her out of the hospital, dragged her across the planet to kill a man she didn't even know, and now brought her back to the States to kill a man she knew better than anyone. Kelly wasn't sure what was left of her soul, but she knew what was left of her journey—two kills. Two presses of a proverbial trigger. One for Reed, and one for her.

Life was a bitch.

"I don't even know what to make of this, Kelly . . ."

Hearing her name broke Kelly out of the fog of hatred consuming her mind and brought her attention back to the present. She blinked and scanned the room, searching for the speaker. It took her a moment to realize that the words were coming from the television mounted against one wall. Her shoulders slumped as her blurry vision settled on the screen. A male news anchor sitting next to a blonde female—*Kelly*, she supposed—gestured with his hands through distorted, flashing images of a burning car with fire engines crowding around it. The caption read *Nashville, TN*. Another image replaced the car fire—this one of a mannequin, dripping in fake blood, hanging from the side of a skyscraper. Kelly recognized the building as 191 Peachtree Tower in downtown Atlanta. Her brow wrinkled, and she blocked out the bustle around her to focus on the TV.

"Are you saying these tragedies are linked?" said Kelly, the reporter.

The male anchor shrugged theatrically. "I mean, who knows, right? It's been a weird two weeks. First, the chaos in Atlanta, then the murder of State Senator Mitchell Holiday in North Carolina. Now a gunfight and car chase in Nashville. This stuff isn't typical, that's all I'm saying. We rarely see this much national news come out of the southeast. Hold on a moment . . . I'm just getting this in from our producers . . ." The man pressed his hand to his ear and hesitated, and then sat up.

"Well, Kelly, maybe I'm not crazy. We've just received an urgent bulletin from the FBI. Take a look at this face, America. A man named Reed Montgomery, apparently a former U.S. Marine, has now been added to the FBI's Most Wanted List. Unconfirmed reports indicate that this man could be wanted in relation to some of the bizarre events we've been discussing today."

The anchor's words faded from Kelly's mind as a black-and-white mug shot covered the screen, showing a man with broad shoulders, defined features, high cheekbones, and a dark stare.

Kelly stared at Reed's face, pretending he was staring right back into her very soul. She tightened her trembling fingers into fists, then got up. Turning away from the television, she walked across the lobby, pushing between the crowds of travelers and security. For eight hours, she sat in the airport, searching her exhausted mind for a next step. Finding a professional killer on the run was the equivalent of locating a needle in a haystack. Reed could be literally anywhere—probably not even in the States—but after seeing his face on the screen, she knew exactly where to look.

She knew Reed, the way he thought, the way he reacted. Reed was a fighter, and a lethal one, but when he was pushed off balance, he always reacted in the same way: he shrank back to whatever felt safe. It was why he called her from the wreckage of the MARTA train outside of Atlanta two weeks before and why he showed up on her doorstep the prior week with his grungy dog in tow. When all else failed, Reed retreated to the last place that felt like home, and now that Kelly was out of the picture, that left only one place.

She dug into the folds of her burka as she stepped up to the ticket counter, producing a fake ID for Samantha Mohammad. It clicked against the counter as her gaze met that of the clerk's.

"One ticket, please," she whispered.

"Yes, ma'am. Where to?"

"Birmingham, Alabama."

# 16

**The Governor's Mansion**
**Baton Rouge, Louisiana**

"You shouldn't be here."

Maggie stood next to the liquor bar, her back turned to Coulier as she poured herself half a glass of red wine. Even with her back turned, she could feel the tension radiating off of her attorney general as he settled onto a wide leather couch in the middle of the mansion's parlor. He was focused—ready for war.

Maggie sat down in one of the wingback chairs that faced the couch and crossed her legs. She wore a loose T-shirt and sweatpants from Walmart—her standard evening attire. Even with a six-figure state salary, Maggie saw little need to upgrade her lifestyle. The wine was cheap, off the shelf of the local grocery store, just the way she liked it. Her makeup was purchased at the Mall of Louisiana, and the simple leather boots she wore on a daily basis were ordered from eBay. Maggie campaigned as one of the people, and she intended to remain that way. The only fancy things that surrounded her were items that predated her administration.

She took a sip of wine and watched Coulier over the top of the glass. The governor's mansion lay quiet, the stillness broken only by the methodical tick of a grandfather clock in the hallway. Maggie didn't like it here—never had. It was stiff, formal, and much too large to ever be cozy, but precedent and security mandated that she make it her home.

"Are you going to explain yourself?" she asked.

Coulier tilted his head. "What do I need to explain?"

"Why you're calling on your single, female governor at her residence at two o'clock in the morning."

Coulier's lips twisted into a dull smile. "Madam Governor, surely you don't so demean yourself as to play into stereotypes of sexually vulnerable female executives."

"No, I don't. But the media does, and in case you haven't picked up a paper lately, there's already some nasty rumors floating around about the incident at my lake house."

Coulier nodded slowly, and Maggie took another sip. She knew he was well informed about the incident. It took place before he was appointed attorney general, but Coulier wasn't the type of man to take a new job while being underinformed about his new boss's appearance in the tabloids. Maggie had snuck away from the governor's mansion unannounced and spent the night at her family's lake house. It was there that a mysterious attacker shot two of her guards before escaping into the night. Maggie claimed it was an assassination attempt, but the gossip columnist had other, less-flattering suggestions about why their female governor was alone with her guards, in a cabin miles from the city.

Maggie tilted the glass, twirling it by the stem until the wine swirled inside like a tiny red hurricane. "It doesn't play well for you to appear without an appointment. Not at my house."

Coulier fingered the leather arm of the couch, then nodded. "I agree, actually. But what I came to discuss is the sort of thing you don't want on the books."

He didn't have to say it. Maggie knew from the moment her gate guard notified her of Coulier's arrival that it wasn't a social call. Coulier wasn't the type to make conversation without some sort of endgame in mind, and any conversation he chose to elicit at two in the morning was sure to be a shady one.

"Maybe I don't want to have the sort of conversation that I wouldn't want on the books." She left the comment open—half question, half statement—waiting to see if he would pick up where she left off.

Coulier nodded slowly, then tilted his head. "I wondered if you might say that. Frankly, that's why I'm here."

Maggie lifted an eyebrow. "To have a conversation about whether I want to have a conversation?"

Coulier interlaced his fingers between his knees. "No. To find out how badly you want to deliver on your campaign promises."

The room became still. Only the ticking of the clock broke the silence as Maggie savored the fading flavor of the wine and watched Coulier's unblinking stare. "What I want, Mr. Attorney General, is to find and destroy the people who are sucking the economic and social vibrancy out of my state. What I want is to find and destroy the people who *threatened my family*."

Coulier rubbed his thumbs against each other, then leaned back into the couch. "A certain . . . *opportunity* has presented itself. An opportunity to shut down the port."

"What is the nature of this *opportunity*?"

Coulier grimaced. "That's the sort of conversation you wouldn't want on the books."

"I see. Is this opportunity an illegal one?"

"Legality is often a grey area, Madam Governor."

"Would this opportunity involve hurting anyone?"

"Only the people you want to destroy. I would advise you not to question me further. I really don't want to create any conversation that I may need to lie about later. Suffice it to say that you gave me an objective—to find a way to close the port. I have found a way. It is somewhat . . . radical, and it will surely land you in some spotlight. But it will get the job done, and when the smoke clears, you'll be a hero."

Maggie drained the glass and set it on the end table. She settled into the overstuffed leather back and imagined she wasn't sitting in a stiff, formal parlor, but was instead nestled into the worn cloth padding of her father's cheap recliner. She imagined that her family was gathered around the living room, drinking beer and staring at the TV as they cheered for LSU, though none of them had ever attended LSU or even set foot on the campus. That didn't matter, it was still their football team. They were proud of it because it was a piece of home. A piece of their culture—a culture that was being badgered and harried by corruption slowly draining the lifeblood from their beautiful state. Ever since Hurricane Katrina, Louisiana had struggled to recover and find her footing again. The Pelican State had been through hell more than once, and nobody had been able to repair the deep wounds left in its soul.

Her family was like so many others in Louisiana—loud, opinionated, fun, hardworking, and resilient. They were fiercely proud of being Louisianan, and they deserved opportunity unhindered by corporate and political corruption. They deserved to be safe and prosperous and unthreatened by men in the shadows.

Men like Gambit.

Maggie walked back to the minibar and poured another half glass of wine, then sighed and made it a full glass. She took a deep sip and spoke without looking over her shoulder. "Do what you have to do, Mr. Attorney General."

Coulier didn't reply, but she heard him stand and walk to the door. It clicked shut behind him, leaving her alone with the tick of the clock and the warmth of the wine. Deep in her soul, a soft voice echoed into her mind —a warning, perhaps, or maybe just a fact.

*"You're at war now."*

# 17

**Fort Morgan, Colorado**

Reed parked the Durango in the back of a Walmart parking lot, nestled into the shadows of decorative trees that shielded him from the glare of overhead lights. While the rear of the SUV appeared to be little worse than battered, the front bore the scars of the gunfight, with a bullet-ridden hood. He would never make it to Alabama without drawing the attention of every cop and highway patrolman over the twelve-hundred-mile route. The Durango would have to be abandoned.

Reed dug his wallet out of his back pocket and produced a hundred dollar bill. "We need water, dry food, and clothes. Wouldn't hurt to have some caffeine pills, if you can find them."

Banks accepted the bill and crammed it into her pocket without a second glance. "What about guns?"

Reed cocked his head. "Say what?"

"Oh, please. I know how your game is played at this point. Sooner or later, we're gonna need guns."

Even though her words were laced with sarcasm, her tone wasn't. She spoke with the monotonous, angry bite Reed had become used to over the last two days. Every word of it stung, sinking into his soul and reminding him that her words used to sound fresh and free, happy and kind, and even a little silly. What had he done to this beautiful woman that she now interpreted her future in terms of weaponry and survival?

"We don't need guns," he said. "At least not from Walmart. I'll sort that out when we get closer. I have a guy."

"Of course you do." She reached for the door handle.

Reed touched her arm, and her blue eyes flashed fire.

"Banks, be careful. If somebody gives you a second glance, if anything at all feels wrong, run out. I'll be waiting."

She sneered. "If anyone gives me a second glance? Guess I need a shower." Banks pulled free from his arm and disappeared into the crowded parking lot.

Reed rubbed a hand across his face, lifted his phone from his pocket, and punched in an all-too-familiar number. After speaking a passcode, the comforting New Orleans drawl of Thomas Lancaster, his private banker, came on the line.

"Good afternoon, Reed. How are you today?"

Reed couldn't resist a smirk. Thomas worked for an underground shell corporation called Lasquo Financial, which presented itself as a financial advisory for wealthy, exclusive businessmen, but was, in reality, the banking front for the criminal underworld. Thomas had managed Reed's dwindling assets for years, and in typical banker fashion, always answered with a warm and professional greeting. Perhaps more remarkable, Reed had never managed to catch the man sleeping. It was as though Thomas sat at his desk 24/7, just waiting to take his call.

"Don't you watch the news, Thomas?" Reed asked. "I think you have a pretty good idea how I'm doing."

There was a pause, and when Thomas spoke again, his words were a little less stiff. "I'm sorry about that, Reed. I'm not sure our services can put the genie back in the bottle."

"No, I wouldn't expect them to. Actually, I'm not calling about money. I need a favor. Something off the books."

"Yes?" Thomas spoke without hesitancy, but there was no commitment in his tone, either.

"Every time I call you, I see a different area code and city on my phone.

Today it looks like I'm calling Baltimore, but last week when I called you, the area code indicated Anchorage."

Silence.

Reed rubbed his lip. "I know you're in New Orleans, so . . ."

"So, you want to know how we make calls appear like they're coming from other parts of the country."

"Well, not actually. What I *actually* want is for you to make *my* call appear that way."

"Reed, I'm in the business of risk mitigation, among other things. Participating in the evasion of federal law enforcement—"

"Thomas, you're a banker. How much will it take to mitigate your risk?"

Silence, again.

"Seriously, Thomas, I need this. Now I can call somebody else and—"

"No, no. Don't start the *other guy* line with me."

Thomas's uncharacteristic snappiness took Reed by surprise, but oddly enough, it also comforted him.

"I'm confident I can speak to our IT department about a solution. Typically, you would call into an internet-based relay service, which then connects your call to a tower in another part of the country before routing it to the person you called. Does that make sense?"

"Yes. So when they trace the call, they source a tower that's miles from where I'm actually sitting."

"Correct. It's not legal, and it's not easy."

Reed smirked. "So, it's not cheap. I get it. How much?"

"Fifteen grand. And this is a one-time arrangement."

"Fair enough. What should I do?"

"Nothing. They'll call you in the next half hour. You'll give them the number you want to speak to and the city you want to appear in. That's all."

"Very good. Thank you, Thomas."

The banker cleared his throat, and his old charisma returned. "Absolutely, Reed. It's always a pleasure to assist one of our *most prestigious* clients."

"You mean most infamous."

"In our business, Mr. Montgomery, the two distinctions are rarely different."

Reed offered his thanks and hung up. He conducted a quick internet search on his phone and wrote down a ten-digit number in the notes app, then took the revolver from the glove box and left the Durango after a careful dusting to displace any fingerprints. It didn't matter. The FBI knew who he was and what he looked like at this point, but perhaps the precaution would delay things a little further when the vehicle was eventually discovered.

It took twenty minutes for Reed to locate a dingy old sedan in the back of a wrecker service's lot half a mile away. As he hoped, the wrecker service was closed, leaving both the gate and the office door locked. There was an old security camera mounted at the corner of the building, staring down into the fenced lot, but no lights blinked beneath the lens, and Reed could see the trailing end of a wire torn free of the wall behind the camera. He couldn't resist another smirk. Stealing a car from a grocery store parking lot would result in a police report within the next few hours, but taking a clearly abandoned vehicle from the back of this wrecker lot might give him as much as six or eight hours.

A speedy application of his lock-picking skills granted him access to the office, and he quickly located the keys to the sedan in an unlocked metal box mounted on a wall. He picked the gate lock, dusted off the windshield, and drove the sedan back to the Walmart in under five minutes. There was less than a quarter tank of gas in the old car, and it squeaked at every turn, but it drove.

*I don't need much—just twelve hundred miles.*

Only moments after parking the car, Reed saw Banks emerge from the Walmart, and he flashed his lights to draw her attention. She hurried over and offloaded an armful of bags into the back seat, then piled in beside him.

"This thing stinks."

"Probably the dead squirrels in the glove box," Reed quipped.

She shot him a glare and settled back into the seat, but Reed didn't move. He checked the time on his cell while tapping one knee. It had been over half an hour since his call with Thomas, and his mind began to wander. The FBI would be closing in on him now, dumping agents into the field and moving highway patrol partners onto the interstates. They'd wrap a net around his possible locations, closing it in until they pinned him down. The only way to escape would be to trick them into moving that net.

Banks opened her mouth, a question hanging in the air, but then the phone buzzed. Reed answered without hesitation but didn't speak.

A soft grunt resounded over the line. "Mr. Montgomery?"

"Who is this?"

"Mr. Lancaster asked me to give you a call."

"Yes. I appreciate your help—"

"What number?" The man was brusque and clearly had better things to do.

Reed read him the number he'd taken down and counted the seconds as his call was put through.

# 18

The florescent lights of the old FBI field office glinted down from overhead, reflecting off dusty computer screens and battered metal desks. Turk's career with the FBI was only a few months old, yet this was the most disorganized and clearly uneventful outpost he had visited. Cheyenne, he guessed, must not see a lot of action, at least on the federal level.

Rollick sat on the edge of a desk, flipping through mounds of paperwork. His hair still dripped from a hot shower he'd just taken, and his glare flashed across each sheet, blazing fire and fury. Turk rubbed his arms and huddled closer to the air vent in the floor. The warm current that pumped its way up his pant legs provided welcome relief to his chilled bones. He could still feel the icy touch of the lake water surging over his body and remember the terror of air rushing from his lungs as blackness closed in around the Tahoe.

*Damn him. Damn Reed.*

By the time Turk had seen the back end of the Durango sitting in the middle of the iced bridge, it was much too late to think. Looking back, he realized he should have never slammed on the brakes. It was the instinctual move of somebody unused to driving in winter weather, and that was exactly what Reed had counted on. He wanted Turk to slam on his brakes.

He wanted the Tahoe to lose traction, spin out of control, and flip over the wall and into the darkness.

Reed always was a fox.

Turk rubbed his hands together. It was probably all in his head, but he couldn't shake the feeling of that biting water closing in around him and sucking him under. For a Marine from Tennessee whose résumé boasted two tours in Iraq and one in Kuwait, nothing about his training had prepared him for the curse of the cold.

Rollick slammed the paperwork down on the table. Anger boiled off the older man like steam from a pot—anger at Turk, anger at their quarry, anger at the field office and its crew of sleepy, lackluster agents. Turk wasn't sure what kind of field agents were assigned to Cheyenne, but he suspected they weren't the young and hungry. No, this place had the feel of a calm retirement office; the place a tenured agent could go to complete his career in peace. Not a bad thing, but not the kind of thing he and Rollick needed at the moment, either.

"Damn you, Turk! Why didn't you shoot him?"

Turk folded his arms. He'd answered this question already, multiple times. He didn't really want to slog through it again. "I missed."

"Sure. You missed. A Marine. A three-tour—"

"A *rifleman*. If I was carrying an M4, I wouldn't have missed."

Rollick snorted and pawed through another two sheets of paper. They were images from the security cameras at the airport. Nothing much to see, really—blurry, black-and-white, and all from bad angles. Of course.

Turk leaned over the table. "Rollick, I'm telling you there's nothing to find in those photos. This isn't about where he's *been*; it's about where he's *going*. We need to know what he's thinking. What his game plan is."

Rollick sneered. "Well, why don't you call him and ask?"

Turk sighed and lifted one finger, but before he could speak, an agent barked from across the room. "Agent Rollick, I think I have your suspect on the line."

Rollick's head snapped up, and he hissed at the room to be silent before he lifted the nearest phone to his ear and nodded once. Turk held his breath.

"This is Special Agent Matthew Rollick, FBI. Who am I speaking with?"

The tendons in Rollick's neck flexed, then he pulled the handset away from his ear and jammed it toward Turk. "He wants to speak to you." The words fell from Rollick's lips in a disgusted sneer.

Turk swallowed, feeling a dry lump fill his throat as his fingers closed around the receiver. Rollick lifted a headset off the desk and settled it over his ears. Every other agent in the room was listening in, also.

Turk settled the handset against his ear, then cleared his throat. "Hello, Reed."

In the background, Turk heard the soft clicking of an agent typing on his computer, frantically working to trace the call.

"Hello, Turk."

The voice hit Turk like a brick in the chest. His mind wavered at the point of memory, and before he could stop himself, he was transported back to Iraq again. That hot July night when he watched Corporal Reed Montgomery disappear into the shadows with a rifle cradled in his arms. Turk stood there, waiting outside the barracks, knowing he should ring up the MPs. Make a panic call. Get somebody's attention.

But he never called anyone. He remained next to the barracks until he heard the distant crack of gunshots blend with the fireworks overhead.

Turk leaned back in the chair. "It's been a long time."

Reed grunted. "That it has. How the hell are you?"

"As it happens, I'm dripping wet and freezing cold."

"Sorry about that. You really should slow down in bad weather."

"I'm an East Tennessee boy, Reed. I don't know anything about driving on icy bridges in Wyoming."

Rollick spun his finger in short air circles, indicating that he wanted Turk to keep Reed talking.

"Reed, I don't know what you're up to, but this won't end in your favor. Trust me. You need to come on in and let me help you."

Reed snorted. "Like you helped me with the court-martial?"

"Reed, you know I couldn't lie. It's not in me. I didn't want you to go to prison. Of course I didn't want you to get the needle. But I was there, Reed. I saw you with the gun. I couldn't lie."

"Sure. You had to tell the truth. And now you're with the FBI . . ."

Turk stiffened. "One thing is not related to the other, Reed. I worked for this job, just like I've worked for everything I've ever had. It sucks to be hunting you down, but you can rest assured, I *will* hunt you down. So don't make this hard on yourself or that girl you're dragging around with you. Come on in, and we can talk."

"You know, I don't think I've got anything to say to the FBI. They seem to think I'm responsible for some attack on a field office in Atlanta."

"Are you?"

"Am I?"

Turk glanced across the room. The agent working the computer waved him away, indicating he needed more time.

"Reed, listen. I never said—"

"No, Turk. You listen." Reed's tone crept from tired indifference to impatience. "None of this is what it looks like. You've known me for a long time, more than most, and you've seen me walk through some serious crap. I don't care what they convicted me of. You know why I killed those men. This is no different than Iraq. So stay out of my way."

Turk could feel Rollick's questioning glare on his back, but he didn't look up. There would be time enough for him to explain himself later. Right now, he needed Reed to keep talking.

"Reed, this isn't about Iraq. This is—"

"This is about today. And today, you are wrong. *Back . . . off.*"

The phone clicked.

Turk cursed and slammed the receiver down, then glared across the room. "Please tell me you got that."

The tracking agent peeled his headset off. He hit a button on his keyboard, and a printer whined to life. Rollick snatched the sheet up and scanned it, his eyes turning cold. The room was silent, and Turk's muscles tensed.

"You said there was a third guy?" Rollick said, still staring at the sheet.

"Huh?"

"A third Marine. On Reed's fire team."

Turk nodded. "Yeah, Johnson. He got shot up and went home."

"Where?"

"What do you mean? Where was he shot?"

"*Where is his home?*"

"Oh. Idaho, I think." Turk started across the room. "Why?"

Rollick handed him the sheet. It was a map, with the address of a cell tower printed at the top.

"Because your boy's headed that way," Rollick said. "He's going to hide out with his old pal."

# 19

**HWY 34 W, Colorado**

"What happened in Iraq?"

The question hung in the air like a gun next to Reed's head. "What are you talking about?"

He decided to play dumb. It wouldn't work, but it felt like the most innocent approach.

"Don't screw with me," Banks snapped. "I'm not the sweet, trusting, innocent little lamb you dragged through the woods in North Carolina. It's time you told me the truth."

Reed adjusted his hips in the worn-out seat. "The truth about what?"

Banks folded her arms. "Everything. Where you came from. Why you're here."

"You want a résumé?"

"I want . . . an explanation." Her voice cracked, and Reed saw red lining her gaze before she turned away. Her cheeks were pallid, and Reed turned the heater up, but he knew she wasn't cold. She was exhausted, strained, haunted.

*I don't talk about this . . . not with anyone.*

The instinctual resistance to discussing his past was as old and dominant as a birth defect. A practiced, protective policy of nondisclosure. He wasn't sure where it began, but the disposition certainly predated Iraq. It probably predated his teenage years.

*And then again, why does it matter? I'm screwed anyway. Doesn't she have the right to know?*

"Why do you care?" Reed asked. Banks didn't care about him, and she certainly didn't care about *them*. So why did she want to know? Maybe she was just bored.

"Doesn't matter. I want to know."

*Fair enough.*

Reed set his elbow on the windowsill and focused on the road ahead. "I was a Marine—"

"Before that." The words cracked like a bullwhip. Reed swallowed. Every time she snapped like this, it stung worse than a fist to his nose. Nothing cut so quick and so deep as her tone. It ripped straight through him.

"Okay, before that. I told you my parents were divorced. My mother moved us to Los Angeles."

"Yes."

"I was in trouble, boosting cars for the gangs. Headed down a bad path. This Marine sergeant showed up, and I don't know, it seemed like a good idea. So, I signed up, and it went well. I was good at being a Marine. They moved me into the Force Recon program—that's like Marine Special Forces."

"I know what Force Recon is."

Again, with the bullwhip.

Reed nodded. "So, I was deployed. First Afghanistan, then when the Iraqi Civil War broke out in 2014, I was sent over there." He waited to see if she would ask for any details, but apparently, she understood that he was glossing over the boring parts. "In Iraq, lots of things happened. I met Turk, the guy I was on the phone with."

"He was a Marine?"

"Yeah, a damn good one. He was on my fire team. Do you know what that is?"

"A group of Marines."

"Right. It was him, me, and this guy from Idaho. He—"

Banks laughed.

"Excuse me?" Reed said.

"Idaho. What a coincidence."

Reed narrowed his eyes. "What does that mean?"

"Oh, nothing. I just know that Idaho is right next to Wyoming. It didn't make sense for you to call the FBI tonight unless you were trying to mislead them. A cynic might think you're setting your Idaho buddy up."

*Damn, she's sharp. Well, no reason to lie about it.*

"I had my call routed through a cell tower in eastern Idaho. They'll pull my file and find out about the other Marine—if Turk hasn't already told them—and they'll assume I'm looking for a friend."

"Smart."

Reed shrugged. "It'll give us a few hours."

He paused, hoping she would give up on her line of questioning, but Banks flicked her fingers in a *get-on-with-it* motion.

*All right. Now for the hard part.*

"So, there was this other Marine, an infantry private. She was attached to our fire team as a Humvee driver during a transport mission. Things went sideways. Johnson was shot up pretty good, and we barely made it out alive. During the course of everything, this private—her name was O'Conner—discovered that a group of civilian contractors stationed in Baghdad was stealing and smuggling antiquities out of Iraq. O'Conner was some kind of artist or historian. Some such thing. She cared about the art and wanted to protect it. She came to me. I guess she trusted me after the firefight . . ." Reed trailed off, staring down the blank highway. There wasn't another pair of headlights in sight, and in the darkness, his mind traveled back all those years to a night just as dark and empty—empty the way her eyes were empty, silent the way her soul screamed.

He was suddenly aware that Banks was staring at him, and he shook his head. The images faded, but the bite of the memory remained. "She . . ." He choked, then looked out his window to avoid Banks's piercing gaze. Before he could change his mind, he decided to just spit it out. "The contractors found out she was going to squeal on them, so they raped and murdered her. I found the body and took care of it." Reed nodded a couple times, then ran his hand over his chin.

Banks's tone didn't soften. "And by 'took care of it,' you mean . . ."

A sudden flash of anger flared deep within him. "I gunned them down like the scum they were. Is that clear enough for you?"

Banks shrugged. There was no mercy or sympathy in her glare. "I don't like implications."

"Fine. I'll make it blunt, then. I was convicted of five counts of first-degree murder and sentenced to death. I was in prison when an underground organization approached me with a chance to get out. If I agreed to perform thirty hits, they would get me off death row. Wipe my slate clean. That was the deal."

"And you took it."

"I'm alive, aren't I? What do you think?"

The anger in her eyes faded into deadness. "Was my godfather one of your hits?"

Reed wrapped his hands a little tighter around the wheel, disguising the tremor that shook them. "Your godfather was my last hit."

"Why didn't you go through with it?"

Reed didn't speak.

She tilted her head, and then a slow realization faded across her face. "We met first, didn't we? That night in the club, back in Atlanta. You had no idea who I was."

Reed couldn't hold back the tears. They welled up in his eyes in spite of his most valiant efforts to blink them away.

Banks snorted a cold, humorless laugh. "Wow. The whole time, you were hunting my godfather. The only good man left in my life. Unbelievable."

Reed whispered, "I *never* would've taken the job had I known."

"Really? You were willing to kill twenty-nine other people to save your own neck, and you want me to believe you'd throw all of that away over me? Please."

"I *did* throw it away over you. The night you visited Mitch in his condo, I was sitting seven hundred yards away, staring through a rifle scope. I never . . ." Reed clenched his teeth. "I *never* wanted you to be hurt. As soon as I realized you were involved, my only goal was to get you out. I kidnapped your godfather to save his life. I left you at the hospital because it was the only way to protect you."

"Protect me? Gee, thanks."

"I had to kill him, Banks! That man at your godfather's cabin? The one who held a gun to your head? He was my old boss. Nothing would've ended until he was dead. I couldn't let you get sucked into that."

"Seriously? Well, nice job on that one, Reed. Because as I remember, I was sucked into it pretty good, as was my godfather. Don't forget, he's still dead!"

"*I can't help that!*" Reed slammed his hand against the dash. "I would have *died* to save his life, but sometimes things don't work out that way. Your godfather may have been nice to you, but he was *not* a good guy. He was tangled up in something dark. Something *messed up*. The same thing that took my father took Mitch, and now it's taken Dick Carter. I don't know what it is, or who it is, or where they are, but you have to see it by now."

A passing car sent blazing pools of light ripping through the cabin, and the orange glow highlighted tear streaks on her face.

Minutes slipped by, dragging against his nerves like nails on a chalkboard, but Reed refused to speak.

When she turned toward him, the open depths of her stare surprised him with its vulnerability. She ran the tip of her tongue over dry lips. "And what are you going to do about it?"

"I'm going to hunt down the bastard responsible, and I'm going to carve his heart out."

# 20

**Marriott Hotel**
**New Orleans, Louisiana**

The thick shades prevented the morning sun from entering the pitch-black executive suite. Gambit's vision blurred as he scrolled through a black-and-white PDF document, laden with rows of narrow text and punctuated by signatures and government seals. After nearly four hours of reading, things were starting to blend together. Nonetheless, everything seemed to be in place.

He rubbed his eyes. His back ached, and his head buzzed, but there was too much work to do. After rubbing the back of his neck to loosen the tense muscles, he speed-dialed one of his favorite contacts and was gratified with an answer on the first ring.

"Gordon."

"Everything is in order. Release the tapes."

"Sure, boss. What about the girl? Fleming said he wants her . . . buried."

"So? Bury her."

Gambit hung up, then walked across the room to his hotel sink and splashed water on his face. A swig of ginger ale washed the stale taste out of his mouth, and he reached for his toes to stretch his constricted muscles.

This job was killing him, one day at a time. But it was worth every sacrifice.

He returned to the desk and ran a hand through his hair, brushing out stray drops of water. He cleared his throat, rolled his shoulders, and took a deep breath.

Now for the plunge.

He picked up the phone again and selected the top contact while nursing his mind off a mental edge of panic. Everything was in order and completed on time. There was nothing to feel edgy about. He should be proud. Aiden would be proud.

The line connected, and Gambit heard the familiar rustle of Aiden's gravelly voice.

"Yes?"

"It's done," Gambit said. He tried to hide the trepidation he felt. "I just received the final documents from the FDA. The drug is approved for distribution."

"Excellent. Was Commissioner Fleming difficult?"

"At first. We showed him the tapes, and he reconsidered his position."

Aiden sighed, and Gambit imagined a wafting cloud of cigar smoke slipping between his boss's lips.

"It's a tragedy, Gambit. The Commissioner of the FDA raping a minor. What is this world coming to?"

Gambit felt the muscles in his chest loosen. "It's a travesty, sir."

"I assume Fleming wanted the tapes?"

"He did. He also wanted the girl removed from the picture."

"And?"

"And I took care of the girl and gave him what I said were the original tapes. Of course, we still have copies."

"Excellent. I look forward to a long and prosperous relationship with the distinguished *Commissioner Fleming*. What about the other thing? The Montgomery issue."

"I spoke with several of Oliver Enfield's former contractors a few days ago. My men installed GPS trackers on their vehicles, so we'll know if they take the bait. If I had to guess, I'd say at least a few of them will take a pass at Montgomery."

"And?"

"I'm not sure. They're good, but Montgomery has a reputation as one of the best. If they knock him off, we can count it as a neutralized liability. If not, Montgomery should be banged up and worn down enough to negotiate."

"Good work, Gambit. Very good work."

The phone buzzed next to Gambit's ear, and he almost choked when he looked at the screen.

"Gambit? Are you there?"

Gambit didn't answer. He jumped up and scooped the TV remote from the nightstand, then flipped through the channels until he landed on a local news station. Maggie Trousdale, the blonde-haired millennial governor of Louisiana, filled the screen. Standing on the darkened steps of the State Capitol, she was illuminated by bright spotlights as a small crowd of politicians gathered around her. An army of reporters pushed in close to her podium as the overwhelmed governor held out her hand and waited for silence.

"Thank you all for coming out on such short notice. I'm here tonight to announce that effective immediately, I am declaring a state of emergency and ordering the closure of the Port of New Orleans to all shipping traffic, foreign and domestic."

Gambit heard Aiden barking his name, and he forced his mind back to the present.

"Gambit! What's going on?"

"Turn on the news," Gambit mumbled.

A roar of questions and outbursts sounded from the crowd of reporters, and Maggie smacked her hand against the podium to silence them. "Just hours ago, I was informed by Port Security that a rare and highly dangerous toxin was discovered in harbor waters. While the exact nature and extent of the pollution are unknown, it is clear to security experts at the port that the safety of shipping operations are in jeopardy, and as such, I am taking the responsible action of closing the port."

This time, the outburst of questions was too much for the governor to silence. The crowd of reporters shouted over one another, competing for attention.

Maggie held up one hand, then gestured toward a reporter from a local station.

"Governor Trousdale, with all due respect, are you *shitting* me?"

Another burst of shouted questions and heated accusations erupted through the speakers.

Maggie screamed for repose and held up one hand. "Everyone! I need you to *listen* if you want me to answer your questions! The security of the people of Louisiana is my utmost concern. I cannot—"

"So, you're just going to cancel our international shipping?"

"Based on currently available data, the safety of harbor personnel and—"

"Do you have any clue how many jobs and—"

Gambit muted the TV. There was no point in listening further. He stood with his feet rooted to the carpet, waiting for Aiden to speak. Each second that ticked by matched a thunderous beat of his heart as sweat began to drain down his back.

Aiden's voice was filled with venom. "It's a ploy. She knows something, or she's fishing. Where is the *Santa Coquina*?"

Gambit rushed back to his computer and flipped through several screens, settling on a satellite view of the Gulf of Mexico. A yellow icon blinked over the water, with a dashed line trailing behind it, all the way back to Colombia. "About ninety miles off the coast. She was going to make port tomorrow afternoon."

"*Shit.*"

The single word ripped through the speaker, and Gambit winced.

"Is her permit cleared?" Aiden asked.

"Yes, but this closure will void that. The shipment won't be allowed entry into New Orleans."

"What other ports can we use? Is Panama City open? Or Mobile?"

"We don't have permits for either port." Gambit forced himself to remain calm in spite of his skyrocketing blood pressure. "It could take over a week to obtain them unless we can get an emergency exception. But with dozens of ships sitting off the coast and unable to make dock in New Orleans, everyone will be looking for an exception."

A crashing sound blasted through the phone. "How did she know?" Aiden screamed. "Do you think there's really a pollution issue?"

As much as Gambit's own fear demanded that he shut down and contain his opinions, his brain took over, commanding him to take control of the conversation. "Not for a moment. She's trying to flush us out, but I'd bet money she's shooting in the dark. The good news is, time is on our side. A hundred lawsuits will be filed against her office before lunch tomorrow. It's only a matter of time before she has to reopen the port."

"We don't *have* time, Gambit. Everything about this business runs on clockwork. The synthetic material on that ship has a lifecycle. Do you understand me?"

"I'm well aware."

"What do we have on Trousdale? We need pressure. *Now*."

"We can't afford that, sir." Even as the words left Gambit's lips, he knew they were bold. Probably too bold. But he had to regain control. "That's exactly what she wants. If we step out now, there's too much risk of exposure. We need to stick to the plan and use Montgomery to deal with the governor."

"How long?"

"I don't know. I'm going to work on getting the *Santa Coquina* rerouted into another port and have the trucks ready to unload her. That's our best bet. Then we deal with Trousdale once and for all."

Aiden didn't reply, and seconds dragged against the frayed edges of Gambit's nerves.

His boss finally grunted, "Call me when it's done."

Gambit hung up and resumed his seat at the desk. Even after a twenty-two-hour day, it was clear he wouldn't be clocking out any time soon.

# 21

**Louisiana State Capitol**
**Baton Rouge, Louisiana**

Even through the thick, bulletproof glass of her office window, the chatter of a few dozen reporters from the courtyard was audible, nagging Maggie's conscience with the panicked outrage of people. She stood next to the curtain and peered down into the streets as the first traces of sunrise bathed the horizon in an orange glow. State policemen lined the sidewalks, holding back the crowds of protestors and angry reporters. In the last hour, the crowd had doubled in size, and even though there were still no more than forty people gathered there, the clenching claws of doubt had settled into Maggie's gut.

What the hell had she done? When the first traces of the heavy lead toxin were discovered in the harbor, the shock and horror of the harbor police and local scientists were her first clue that she had drastically overstepped her bounds. Coulier's scheme—this drastic, mindless, madman scheme to shut down the harbor—had always felt extreme. But now, standing in the window, reading the waving signs of the now jobless harbor workers, the reality of her decision began to sink in.

"What do I do now?" she whispered.

The door burst open behind her, slamming back on its hinges with all the force and noise of a shotgun blast. Maggie spun around, her heart skyrocketing into her throat.

Dan Sharp stood in the doorway, his face washed white with stress, fear, and God knew what else. He wasn't wearing a coat or tie, and his shirt was stained with sweat. "Maggie, what the hell have you done?"

"Shut the door, Dan." Maggie forced herself to remain calm. The ends of her nerves were as frayed and worn as her body, now sleepless for the past thirty hours, but her better sense took over, at last, and kept her from screaming at him. Dan shoved the door shut and stomped across the room.

Before he could explode again, Maggie gestured to a chair. "Sit down. Breathe. You need a drink."

She walked across the room and reached for a decanter of brandy, but Dan didn't sit.

"Maggie, what are you *doing*?"

Maggie poured herself a glass and took a long sip of the stinging beverage. It barely served to take the edge off. More than anything, she just needed something to do with her hands. "I did what I had to do, Dan."

"You dumped *chemical waste* into the Port of New Orleans! Are you out of your *mind*?"

"Chemical waste? Who told you that?"

Dan jabbed his closed knuckles at her, the way politicians do. "Don't play coy with me, Maggie. What did Coulier say? That he could *rustle up an emergency*? Less than two days later, you have the Coast Guard close the port because toxic waste is discovered at the docks. Are you kidding me? Maggie, this is *criminal*!"

Maggie set her jaw. She wasn't sure if her fear or frustration was taking precedence. Maybe it was neither—maybe it was just exhaustion. Either way, she was sick of it.

"Sit *down*, Dan!"

She slammed her glass against the brandy table and stomped across the room. Dan crumpled into the chair with a shocked, unsettled look crossing his face.

Maggie leaned across the desk. "I don't know who you've been talking to, but you will *not* launch angry, mindless accusations at me. I'm doing what I need to do to fix this state. What the people *hired* me to do. If you don't have the *guts*—"

"The *guts*? The guts to be *corrupt?*"

"Don't you *dare* use that word with me!"

Dan's eyes blazed, and he sat bolt upright. "Oh, I will use that word because that's my *job*. What you're doing right now is wrong, illegal, and dangerous. You're putting *thousands* of people out of work, poisoning the port, costing the state millions of dollars, and sabotaging your own administration over a *hunch*. I told you from the start, Coulier was a mistake. A wretched, foolish, deadly mistake. But you wanted to go ahead with it. You wanted a pit bull. Well, you got it, Maggie. You got your pitbull. And now he's off his chain and rampaging through the city, leaving chaos and carnage everywhere he goes. What do you want, Maggie? What's the plan here?"

"To cleanse this state of corruption!"

"By *being* corrupt?" Dan almost screamed the question.

"Sometimes you have to fight fire with fire, Dan."

*"Bullshit.* That's exactly the sort of crap you campaigned against. Are you totally blind?"

Maggie collapsed into the chair, trying to pretend she wasn't sitting in the State Capitol and that she wasn't the governor. She tried to imagine that she was still gigging frogs and hunting alligators with her brother in the bayous. But as hard as she tried, there was no relief from the crushing weight of reality. She couldn't escape it anymore.

"I think you had better go home, Dan."

Dan's gaze, so full of fury only moments before, was now traced by hurt.

Maggie didn't care. She couldn't afford to care.

"Are you sure about that?" he asked.

She nodded once, impassive.

He rose. "All right, then. Madam Governor, effective immediately, I resign my position as lieutenant governor of this state. You can expect my resignation letter within the hour."

Maggie sat up. There was resolve in his words, still pained, still hurting, but ironlike nonetheless.

A sudden uncertainty crept into her mind, mixing with the shock of his words. “Dan, you’re not doing that. I need you now more than ever. Perhaps I’m overreacting. Don’t take this personally.”

“I’m not, Maggie. If I was taking it personally, I’d shove you through that window. I’m doing what the people hired me to do. I’m telling you the truth. And if you won’t let me do my job, there’s no reason for me to be here anymore. I’m done.”

“Dan, this state needs—”

“This state *needs* character. And you have become exactly what you swore to fight. I will not—”

The door burst open. Once again, the room resounded with the clap of wood against wood and the screech of abused hinges. Coulier appeared, a single sheet of paper flapping from his outstretched hands. His face was strained with exhaustion, but excitement danced like fire in his eyes. He met Dan’s gaze, and fire clashed with fire. Dan moved to intercept him, but Coulier sidestepped and slammed the paper onto the table.

“The *Santa Coquina,* a one-hundred-thirty-meter Panamanian-flagged cargo ship. She left port in Barranquilla, Colombia, three days ago, with a destination of New Orleans. Since you closed the port, she has filed *eleven* emergency port entry applications. The cargo? Bananas.”

Maggie saw a flash of uncertainty cross Dan’s gaze.

She turned back to Coulier. “What are you saying?”

A small smile crept across the attorney general’s lips. “What I’m saying, Madam Governor, is that we took a shot in the dark. And we hit something.”

# 22

**Colby, Kansas**

The sun broke over the windshield, exposing the vast emptiness of west Kansas desolation. Reed had never been to Kansas and was amazed by the sheer emptiness of it all. It wasn't perfectly flat, but the wide-open plains dotted with windmills came damn close. With nothing to block the sun, the glare in his face brought on a headache almost immediately.

Banks sat beside him, silent and brooding. She hadn't slept all night, and her bloodshot eyes were now rimmed with dark circles. Reed glanced down at the fuel gauge, then changed lanes to take the next exit. By his best estimate, another fourteen hours of hard driving lay between them and north Alabama, and they had to stop in Mississippi to refit first. It was going to be a long day.

"We need to load up on some caffeine and refuel. You should eat."

Banks nodded. Reed turned onto a two-lane highway that shot upward toward Colby, Kansas. A single fuel station a mile distant had a dusting of snow scattered around it. An old Chevy truck was parked out back, but there were no other customers. That was good.

The car squeaked to a stop next to the pump, and Banks immediately put her hand on the door latch.

Reed instinctively grabbed for her door handle. "Where—"

"I have to pee," she snapped.

Banks walked across the lot and into the small station, where a solitary man leaned next to the counter. He looked up as she passed, his gaze lingering longer than Reed would have liked.

*Worn out, dirty, and still a knockout.*

Reed pried himself out of the car and twisted his back until it cracked. His whole body ached. Even his ass felt like somebody had beaten it with a baseball bat. The thought brought a strange, fleeting smile to his face as he recalled the late nights in Los Angeles spent boosting cars with other gangster wannabes. Back then, he never would've wasted time on a piece of junk like the rusty sedan behind him. He never would've settled for less than two doors and four hundred horsepower.

*Amazing how times change.*

The glass door of the fuel station squeaked. Reed kept his head low as he approached the counter and dropped thirty bucks in front of the attendant.

"Pump two," he muttered.

The attendant laughed. "Yeah. You're the only one out there. Anything else?"

Reed hesitated, then sighed. "Yeah. Pack of Marlboros. Make it two packs, and a lighter."

The man grunted and dropped the cigarettes on the counter. Reed thumbed out another ten-dollar bill, then scooped up the merchandise and turned toward the door. As he did, a dull squeak resounded. Maybe it was the bathroom door, but the footfall was too heavy to be Banks—too hard to be anything other than a boot.

*Click.*

The metallic sound ripped across the room a split second before Reed dove for the floor. A chorus of suppressed gunshots filled the air in a series of sharp *pops*, and a bag of chips exploded over Reed's ear, sending an avalanche of nacho cheese crumbles raining over his neck. He clawed beneath his jacket for the grip of the revolver he'd taken from Carter's secretary. The weapon cleared his belt as he rolled onto his back, exposing the man who circled the corner of the aisle, holding a silenced pistol extended in one hand. He was taller than Reed, maybe six-seven, with broad shoulders and a massive head obscured by a ski mask.

Reed jerked the trigger of the revolver, but his shot flew wide as the killer twisted to his left and aligned the muzzle of his weapon with Reed's forehead. Reed pulled the trigger again, and this time the revolver clicked over an empty chamber.

*Shit.*

"Hey, you!" The attendant's voice boomed from behind the counter, mixed with the familiar *schlick-schlick* of a pump-action shotgun. Gunfire exploded on all sides as Reed ducked for cover amid a shower of glass and ruptured Gatorade bottles. Somebody screamed, and he heard what sounded like the shotgun clattering to the floor, but he didn't wait to see where it fell.

Twisting the revolver in his hand until he gripped the weapon by the barrel, Reed launched himself across the aisle and slammed the butt of the gun into the big man's temple. The two of them crashed to the ground as the silenced pistol spun beneath a shelf, momentarily out of reach. Cans of soup, bags of candy, and toilet paper rained over the floor, mixing with a growing pool of cheap beer as they rolled into a deathlock. Reed slammed his hand upward, connecting with his attacker's jaw forcefully enough to dislocate it. Bone cracked against bone, then a blunt forearm snapped against Reed's nose, sending his head cracking against the tile floor.

The big man climbed off of him, ripped off his ski mask, and exposed an ugly face smeared with sweat.

Reed kicked his way backward. The face hanging almost seven feet overhead was broad, ugly . . . and familiar. "Cowboy?" Reed spoke past a growing pool of blood in his mouth.

A grin spread across the big man's lips as he reached beneath his jacket and produced a backup gun. "Wassup, Prosecutor?"

Reed's fingers landed on the nearest item of fallen merchandise—a can of sausages—and he slung it toward the leering head with as much force as he could muster. He missed, and the muzzle of the handgun rose over his face.

Cowboy snorted. "Adios, amigo."

Banks came hurtling over a low shelf, a wooden-handled toilet plunger raised over her shoulder like a baseball bat. Momentary confusion flashed across his face as Cowboy began to turn, but not before the business end of the plunger collided with his face, sending a cascade of sordid water spraying over Reed.

Banks landed on both feet like a cat and swung again, whacking her victim over the stomach this time. Cowboy cursed and struggled to swat away the harmless rain of blows from Banks's puny weapon, but she kept swinging.

Rage clouded Cowboy's eyes as he swung a meaty arm to intercept the next swing of the plunger. Banks overreached and began to stumble as the killer raised his handgun, poised to deliver a gutshot.

The next can of sausages struck home in Cowboy's left eye. Reed jumped to his feet, a third can clenched in his hand, as he hurled himself across the narrow aisle and drove his loaded fist into the big man's rock-hard stomach. Cowboy squeezed off a single gunshot, but the bullet flew wide as Reed sent them both crashing to the floor.

Another strike to the face. The handgun hit the floor, and Reed slammed his knee into Cowboy's groin. A satisfying scream of pain erupted, and Reed grabbed the first metal thing he could find: a corkscrew-style anchor, designed to restrain small dogs.

The polished tip of the implement plummeted toward the big man's neck, but he was too quick, slipping to the side in time to avoid the stab. Reed choked as a fist collided with his stomach, and he crumpled to the floor again. Banks reappeared at the end of the aisle, the plunger replaced with the broken neck of a glass bottle. As Reed's shoulder blade collided with the tile floor, Banks threw herself on the big man's back and thrust out with the bottle, slamming the sharp edge into his exposed neck. Cowboy roared and clawed at the bottle as fresh blood spilled into Reed's face. With all the force he could muster, he slung the big man off of him, back into the toppled shelf, and pulled himself to his feet. Cowboy slung Banks off as though she were a sack of groceries, and he scrambled to his feet. Long before he reached a kneeling position, Reed retrieved the backup gun and trained the sights on his face.

The chaos that ruled the small store faded away and the two men locked eyes. Scars patterned the assassin's features, with one eye swollen shut, but it was still a face Reed would have recognized anywhere.

Reed tilted his head and breathed a ragged sigh. "Really?"

Cowboy sighed, his smile twisted with irony. "Sucks, doesn't it? I always liked you, Prosecutor."

"I'll bet you did. I saved your *life* in Morocco."

Cowboy shrugged. "Two million is two million."

"Is that what I'm worth? Who the hell hired you?"

Cowboy just smirked.

Reed placed his finger on the trigger. "You know what? I don't even care. Go to hell, you backstabbing bastard."

Cowboy held up a hand. "Do what you've got to do, Prosecutor. But first, you should probably know . . ."

Reed glared. "What?"

"Zeus is outside."

Reed heard the distant snap of a rifle shot before the last word left Cowboy's lips. He folded his right knee and dove to the floor as the glass behind his head exploded under the impact of a heavy-caliber sniper round. Cowboy erupted into a laugh and reached for the knife strapped to his side, but before his fingers wrapped around the hard plastic, Reed retrained the sights against his face and fired. Once. Twice. The bold features exploded as the big assassin from Oklahoma crumpled against the shelf.

Another rifle shot split the room, sending cascades of glass over the floor. Banks shrieked and huddled behind the fallen shelf. Reed army crawled around the fallen piles of merchandise, reaching her only a moment later as the third bullet tore through a soda cooler ten feet away.

"Banks! We have to move!"

Banks lay in a fetal position with both hands curled around her head, blood seeping from half a dozen minor cuts on her arms. Her whole body shook.

"He'll shoot us!" she screamed.

"Not if we get to the car first. I need you to trust me."

He grabbed her hand, and their eyes locked.

"He's not here for you, Banks. He's here for me. Follow my lead, and you'll be fine."

Reed twisted around the end of the shelf, surveying the fuel pumps where the sedan sat untouched by the gunfire. They would never make it that far without being cut down.

*The truck.*

Reed led Banks by one hand, worming their way toward the counter. The attendant on the floor had a bullet hole drilled perfectly through the center of his forehead, and the shotgun lay beside him, but Reed ignored it. He would need much more than a shotgun to face the sniper outside. Zeus, Oliver's ex-Greek Special Forces assassin, was so named both for his nationality and his penchant for what he called the 'Thunder of God'—overpowered sniper rifles. The man rarely missed, and when he hit, there was very little left over to tell the tale.

The only way to beat a sniper? Get close. *Really close.*

Reed pressed his hands into the attendant's pocket and dug around until he produced a key labeled with a Chevrolet bow tie.

*The truck out back was a Chevy. There's got to be a back door.*

"This way!" Reed hissed. The gunshots had ceased for the moment, but only because Zeus couldn't see beneath the low block wall that framed the now-shattered windows. He would wait, Reed knew. He'd wait for The Prosecutor to poke his head up, searching for an escape.

*He can't have that chance.*

Reed pulled Banks behind the counter and pushed the shotgun into her hands. "Do you know how to use this?"

She nodded several times, clutching the weapon to her chest.

He squeezed her hand and offered what he hoped was a reassuring smile. She didn't appear in any way calmed.

"Good. You won't have to. I'll be right back, okay? Stay behind the counter."

Reed turned for the open door to the store's office but felt Banks's hand snag his sleeve. He stopped, and her lips parted.

"Reed . . . I'm sorry. I never meant—"

Reed squeezed her hand. "I know. Stay down now."

A quick twist of the latch and the back door squeaked open on frozen hinges. A blast of icy air penetrated the store, and Reed pulled himself into a crouch.

Ten feet away, the Chevrolet was parked next to the building with the cab safely sheltered from the wrath of the sniper. Reed walked in a crouch to the truck, unlocking the passenger door and worming his way in while remaining beneath the windows.

*God, I hope this thing starts.*

The moment the engine turned over, the gunfire resumed. Reed shoved the truck into reverse while lying on his stomach across the bench seat. The tires spun as he pushed his right fist against the gas pedal, then the truck shot backward, away from the station, and into the empty plains. A bullet hit the front fender but failed to strike the engine block as Reed shoved the shifter into drive and hit the gas again. More bullets struck the front of the truck, zipping through the windshield and slamming into the roof of the cab. Reed jerked the bottom of the steering wheel back and forth as the pickup cleared the roadway and hit the open ground beyond. A sharp hiss exploded from the radiator as a sniper round tore through it, but the engine was in no danger of overheating in the next thirty seconds.

Reed pried himself into a seated position and shoved his foot against the gas while keeping low, one eye above the dash, as he swerved around a shallow ditch.

The next gunshot gave away Zeus's position—fifty yards ahead behind a shallow rise. Reed swung the truck directly toward him and rammed his foot into the floorboard. The engine roared as snow exploded into the air, and another panicked rifle shot split the air, sending a bullet through the truck's roof. Reed spun to the right, missing a follow-up shot with mere inches to spare, then jerked back to the left, centering the bumper right at the camouflaged mound of the sniper.

Zeus never stood a chance. He leapt to his feet, abandoning the rifle as he made a frantic dash to the left. Reed followed him with the truck, bracing himself against the dash as the bumper collided with flesh and bone. A sickening *thunk* shook the cabin as the truck hopped over the human obstacle and spun to a stop. Reed choked on wind and dirt as he clawed Cowboy's backup gun out of his waistband and clambered out of the truck. Snow settled around him in a gentle shower, blending now with pools of red as Reed stumbled across a shallow ditch and raised the gun.

There was no need. Zeus lay on his side in the snow, his face twisted into a permanent grimace of agony. Wide tire tracks crossed his collapsed chest, and a growing red stain gathered around his pelvis.

Reed lowered the gun, staring down at the face a long moment more. The wind sucked the energy from his body, leaving him standing alone over the remains of a former colleague.

With a weary sigh, Reed pressed the pistol back into his waistband and lumbered toward the fuel station.

# 23

**Six Miles off the Louisiana Coast**

Waves erupted on all sides of the RB-M as the forty-five-foot boat rocketed over the surface of the Gulf, cutting its way southbound at a speed of just under forty knots. The American flag snapping in the wind over the pilothouse flew inches above the Coast Guard flag, proudly declaring the ownership of the vessel.

Lieutenant Junior Grade Zach Jackson stood in the middle of his thirteen-man boarding party at the aft of the RB-M, while the three-man boat crew scurried about the helm, trimming their approach on the freighter. With every wave, a spray of icy water blasted him in the face, but Jackson didn't mind. Compared to his last post off the coast of Portland, Maine, Louisiana was a dream job. Even at this time of year, the water was hardly cold for him, and it was a great deal calmer, too. He could deal with the muddy Mississippi and more frequent boarding missions in exchange for not freezing his ass off every time he put to sea.

The boat's jet engine groaned over a swell, and Jackson felt a gentle prod in his elbow.

"There!" One of the boarding party standing at his side pressed a pair of binoculars into his hand, and Jackson peered through them across the horizon. Sure enough, barely a mile distant and churning a bat-out-of-hell course southeast, the small Panamanian freighter appeared through the misted lens of the binoculars. Jackson couldn't see any of the crew topside, but that wasn't unusual. From the aft of the 130-meter ship, Panama's flag flapped in the breeze just above the eloquently painted name, *Santa Coquina.*

Jackson handed the binoculars back to the man at his elbow and shouted over the wind. "Lock and load!"

Each of the thirteen-man boarding party drew his SIG Sauer .40 caliber handgun and checked to make sure it was chambered and ready for action. Four of the boarding crew also carried Remington 870 shotguns, and the air resounded with the sharp *schlick-schlick* of fresh shells being pumped into the chambers.

The men huddled around Jackson were members of MSST—the Coast Guard's Maritime Safety and Security Team. Boarding questionable vessels churning their way off the United States coast was one of their many specialties, and Jackson had conducted a full dozen such boardings in the weeks since transferring to the Gulf. The MSST here was more practiced and mechanical than the one he left behind in Portland—probably because of the extreme volume of shipping that passed in and out of New Orleans. Jackson had been altogether pleased with their performance. He was even more satisfied to note that none of the men standing around him reflected any of the nervousness he knew they felt. That nervousness wouldn't be because of the boarding, as this boarding would be no different than the half-dozen others they completed that month. No, these men were tense because of the chemical waste scare and closed port behind them, a drastic and unusual event that had sent the entire Coast Guard Sector spinning in a cloud of special missions and additional security needs.

"Stay sharp!" Jackson called out. "I need everybody on point."

The RB-M rolled to one side, bobbing on the surface as the motor died down. Jackson waved two fingers at the bosun's mate, who maintained command of the vessel. The mate nodded back, then lifted the radio off its security clip above the helm. Jackson could hear his voice boom over the roar of the engine as they continued to close on the freighter.

"Attention, *Santa Coquina,* this is the United States Coast Guard. Under

Title Fourteen of the U.S. Code, we have the authority to board your vessel for a routine search. Halt your engines and lower your accommodation ladder."

The muscles in Jackson's back tensed as the RB-M swayed beneath him. He squinted across the horizon at the growing mass of the *Santa Coquina* and waited for the surf behind her stern to slow as she ceased her course southward. The moments drained into minutes.

"Come on . . . not today."

This was a routine search. Nothing special. Sure, Jackson had been ordered to report back to the Sector Commander immediately upon completion of his search, which was somewhat unique. And the original request to search the vessel was made by the governor of Louisiana, which was a lot more unique. But Jackson didn't care about all that. His job was to board the freighter and complete his search without anyone being hurt. Noncompliance by the commander of the *Santa Coquina* would be worse than a headache—it would be a full-scale emergency. The director of Homeland Security would be on the line long before Jackson ever made it back to New Orleans.

"Not today," Jackson repeated. "Don't make me the guy who triggers a national emergency."

He accepted the binoculars from the man at his elbow, then sighed in relief as he saw the *Santa Coquina*'s wake subside and the accommodation ladder fall down the side of the freighter.

He handed the binoculars back and checked his SIG. The weapon was chambered and ready. Not that Jackson expected to need it, but it was in his nature to be prepared.

"All right. Gibs, Hunt, you've got the engine room. Yates and Giles, you take steerage. Bullock and Meeks, you've got the helm. Everybody else, with me."

The RB-M's water-jet engine began to wind down as the bosun's mate piloted the craft alongside the *Santa Coquina.* As they drew closer to the freighter, Jackson marveled again at just how big it was. Sure, for a freighter, the *Santa Coquina* was actually pretty small, but compared to the small fishing boats he was used to boarding off the coast of Maine, everything about this ship impressed him. How the hell did a ship like this even float?

The RB-M hummed to a full stop, and the bosun's mate piloted the drifting craft expertly next to the freighter. A moment later, the accommodation ladder was latched to the boat, and Jackson pointed two fingers at the vessel.

The MSST dispersed toward the ladder with smooth, practiced ease. Gibs and his Remington shotgun took point, scurrying up the ladder only inches above Hunt. The two of them would rush immediately to the engine room of the *Santa Coquina,* securing the controls, while Yates and Giles repeated the procedure in the steerage room, and Bullock and Meeks took tactical control of the helm. The process was designed to ensure that nobody aboard the *Santa Coquina* could make any attempt to move the freighter while the remainder of the MSST searched the vessel—standard procedure for any boarding.

The polymer rungs of the ladder clicked under the soles of Jackson's boots as he propelled himself up the side of the craft. Two of his men stood at the bulkhead, shotguns held across their chests, as four Hispanic crewmen huddled in a tight circle ten feet away, confusion and trepidation clouding their faces.

"Who's the captain?" Jackson asked.

One of the MSST members gestured toward the shortest, heaviest of the crewmen. "I think it's him, sir. Not certain."

Jackson grunted and stepped forward. "Are you the captain of this vessel? *El capitán*?"

The man nodded several times.

"Very good. I'm Lieutenant Junior Grade Jackson of the U.S. Coast Guard, here to perform a routine search of your vessel as authorized by Title Fourteen of the U.S. Code. Do you understand?"

Jackson suspected that he *did* understand by the glint in his eye and the fact that he offered no protests to the MSST members crawling around his ship, but the captain was playing dumb. Well, that was fine.

"Juarez!" Jackson called over his shoulder.

The Honduran-American petty officer appeared at his side, already repeating Jackson's declaration in Spanish. The captain still played dumb, but at that point, Jackson didn't care. He'd been given every courtesy. It was time to get the job done.

Jackson snapped his fingers, and one of the MSST members appeared from an open door that led inside the boat.

"We've cleared the vessel, sir. Petty Officer Meeks has command of the helm, and we're reviewing ship's logs and licenses now for compliance. It's a reefer freighter. All cargo is refrigerated inside the hold."

Jackson turned back to Juarez. "Ask him what cargo he's hauling."

Juarez gestured to the hold and rattled off a short string of Spanish.

Jackson's Spanish wasn't strong, but *bananas* sounded the same in both languages. "Is that all?" Jackson demanded.

"Just bananas," Juarez said.

Jackson scanned the length of the ship. "That's a lot of bananas, Captain."

Juarez queried the now-chatty captain for a few moments, then shrugged. "He says they're only half loaded. He says business is difficult in Colombia."

"I'll bet it is," Jackson muttered. "Ask him if there's anything on board I should be aware of. Ask him firmly."

Juarez snapped the question as more of a demand than an inquiry, and the captain shook his head adamantly.

"Just bananas," Juarez said again.

"All right." Jackson waved the captain aside. "Well, let's have a look. Tell him to open the hold."

The captain moved toward the center of the freighter without hesitation, motioning Jackson to follow. The MSST maintained a perimeter around Jackson and Juarez, guarding the other three crew members while the captain approached the control module that operated the hydraulic liftgate over the main hold. The captain continued to chat in Spanish while he flipped switches on the face of the module and gestured at the hold.

"He's talking about shipping frustrations," Juarez said. "They were bound for New Orleans when the port was closed. He said the bananas will be ripe soon, and if he doesn't find a port to offload in, his cargo will be ruined, and he'll lose his job."

"Where were they headed in such a hurry?"

A brief interchange between Juarez and the captain resulted in a grunt from the petty officer. "He doesn't know. He received directions from his boss to navigate eastward. They were filing emergency port certificates with Mobile and Panama City."

The hum of a hydraulic pump whined over the deck of the ship, and the captain pressed a button on the module. A shrieking grunt ripped over the deck, and the giant door of the cargo hold began to creep open. Jackson stepped forward and lifted a flashlight from his belt as the first crack of darkness opened beneath the rising door.

# 24

**Coast Guard Sector Command**
**New Orleans, Louisiana**

Maggie leaned low over the desk and bit her lip. The speakerphone next to her remained silent, and she checked her watch. Captain Willis Beech, the Coast Guard Sector Commander for New Orleans, as well as the captain of the Port of New Orleans, sat behind the desk. He too watched the phone, but his face remained blank and impassive—a look Maggie was now used to after the last day of hourly interactions with Beech. As captain of the port, it was Beech who had closed New Orleans after the discovery of toxins at the pier. As far as the Coast Guard was concerned, Beech was God when it came to New Orleans. He maintained complete control of the port, as well as the thousands of miles of complex coastline in and around New Orleans. He'd taken some convincing when Maggie first suggested that the port be closed, and even more convincing when she requested a foreign-flagged vessel be boarded and searched without any specific, concrete reason or evidence, especially given all the chaos and drama he was dealing with over the closure of the port.

But foreign-flagged or no, the *Santa Coquina* was well within the coastal waters of the United States, which made boarding it a somewhat inconsequential and routine thing to do. In spite of Dan's trepidation and Maggie's own jeopardy, after meeting with Coulier the night before over the emergency port documents filed by the *Santa Coquina,* Maggie had made a choice to bring Beech in on her private war, at least as much as was necessary to board the vessel. She wasn't worried about Beech asking too many questions—the captain was literally swamped, and she had little concern that he would find any connection between the closure of the port and the abnormal request of a state governor to board the vessel.

"How much longer?" Maggie asked.

Coulier was cool as a cucumber beneath the gentle breeze of a ceiling fan. Dan wasn't in attendance due to his inability to keep a level head.

Beech grunted. "Just a moment, Madam Governor. They're searching the ship now."

Maggie resisted the urge to pace. Typically, she would be the one sitting behind the desk, maintaining her cool while Dan freaked out. But today, after all that had happened, it was impossible not to feel the strain.

What had she done? Had she lost her mind, participating in Coulier's wild, illegal scheme to close the port and flush out . . . *who*, exactly? Some faceless bad guys? She wasn't sure why it seemed like such a logical idea when Coulier first proposed it. Now, two days later, with fallout exploding all around her, Dan's point of view felt more reasonable by far.

But it was too late now. She was invested. In over her head. The only thing she could possibly do was kick for the surface and hope like hell that this ship was the smoking gun she needed it to be.

A crackle of static flowed from the speaker. Lieutenant Jackson was patched into the office through his radio.

"Captain Beech, this is Jackson. We've completed our search of the vessel."

"And?" Beech asked.

"Nothing out of the ordinary, Captain. The ship is poorly maintained and could certainly be issued some safety citations, but the logs and the cargo are in order. It's carrying a few tons of green bananas. The captain tells me his company filed the emergency port entry requisitions because they'll lose the cargo if the bananas go ripe before they reach port."

Maggie felt her heart drop to her shoes like a lead weight. The room swayed around her, and she gripped the desk. Without pausing to allow her better judgment to take over, she blurted, "Are you *sure*?"

The line was silent, then Beech cleared his throat. "Lieutenant, you're on with Governor Trousdale."

Another pause and Jackson coughed. "Um, good morning, Madam Governor. I didn't realize you were on the line."

"Are you *sure*, Jackson? Are you sure the cargo is clear?"

"We'd need to unload and disassemble the ship to be absolutely certain, but with respect, Madam Governor, that's not logistically plausible at this time. With all the certainty I can offer under the circumstances, the ship is clean."

Maggie dug her fingernails into the captain's desk. Beech stared at her with his head tilted.

Maggie sighed. "Very good, Lieutenant. You may release the ship and return to port."

Jackson garbled a few acknowledgments, and then the line went dead.

The irritation and condescension that blanketed Beech's face was dampened by no hint of restraint. Maggie had found the Sector Commander to be completely professional and cooperative up to this point, but she had no doubt he was reaching his limits.

"Captain, I'm sorry. We have evidence that there *is* something—"

Beech cut her off for the first time. "Evidence of *what*, exactly, Madam Governor?"

She opened her mouth to fill the question with a vague excuse, but he cut her off again.

"I just sent a fully armed, highly trained team of expensive professionals to board a ship for no apparent reason. Meanwhile, the whole city is going to hell due to this port closure. I've got the mayor blowing up my office, and half a dozen big-name law firms from out of state representing major shipping interests threatening lawsuits if the port isn't opened. On top of all that, we've got a legitimate, major concern of unprecedented pollution at the dockside. I hope you'll forgive me for being so direct."

Maggie straightened and plowed through her tired mind, looking for a reason, any reason, why boarding the ship was a legitimate move and not a bad hunch. There was nothing she could say that would hold water if

Beech pressed her, and she knew it. The fact remained—she ordered the ship searched on a desperate suspicion, and that was something she couldn't admit to. When Coulier brought her evidence of a ship loaded with bananas that was filing an inordinate number of emergency port entry applications, the evidence seemed so clear—so damning. Why would a banana freighter be so desperate to make port? There hadn't seemed like any legitimate explanation at the time, and yet, the one given by the vessel's captain was so simple and so obvious.

The freighter needed to make port before the bananas became overripe. How could she have possibly overlooked that? How could all three of them have overlooked that?

"I'm sorry, Captain." Maggie faced Beech, her hands trembling with frustration. "I can't discuss my investigation at this time. I appreciate your generous cooperation."

The veins in Beech's neck twitched, and his cheeks flushed. Maggie knew he felt like a fool. Pissing off the Coast Guard's most powerful local officer while serving as governor of a state with almost eight thousand miles of coastline was the last thing on her agenda. But she couldn't unspill the milk now. The only thing she could do was maintain authority.

Without another word, Maggie turned around and pushed through the heavy wooden doors of the office. A few steps later found her outside in the brisk fall air, where her detail waited, along with Coulier and Dan. She didn't speak a word to either of them until they were safely within the confines of her armored Tahoe, leaving her driver and detail outside.

Dan couldn't hold himself back any longer. "*Well?*"

Maggie flinched and wished she were anywhere else. "Nothing. They found nothing. Just bananas."

The silence of the Tahoe was total. Almost deathly calm, like the sinister stillness of a New Orleans cemetery. Then Dan snapped. She could see it in his face, like his nerves were a rubber band stretched too far, for too long, and now they just broke apart.

"I'm done. I'm done, dammit! I won't take part in this anymore!"

Dan threw the door open and leapt out of the Tahoe before either Maggie or Coulier could stop him.

"Madam Governor—"

"This was *your doing*!" Maggie almost screamed the words, whirling on Coulier and spitting them in his face.

The attorney general recoiled toward the wall, but his features remained placid. Unfazed.

"You conniving son of a bitch. I should have listened to Dan from the start. I should have never hired you!"

Maggie let her face collapse into her hands. She could hear the distant chanting of protestors gathered around the Coast Guard Sector Headquarters, screaming their outrage at the closure of the port, screaming their outrage at their governor. Each chant tore through Maggie's body, breaking her down.

She reached for the door handle as the realization sank into her tired mind: it was time to make all of this right—to come clean and face the people.

Coulier's hand touched her knee. She was surprised by the strength of his grip. She turned toward him, her blood already boiling, but his calm words froze her where she sat.

"There comes a time in every story where a hero makes a choice. Do the easy thing, or do the right thing. If you step out that door and do what you're thinking about doing, it may feel like the right thing, but it's not. It's the easy thing. Those people out there need a hero—somebody who will do what she said she was going to do and cleanse this state of corruption. The path isn't pretty, and it isn't clean. But it's a path *you* promised to follow. If you quit now, you're no better than the people you swore to destroy."

She gritted her teeth. "I *am* the people I swore to destroy. Thanks to *you*. Don't try to save your skin by—"

"My skin is already saved. If you step through that door, I'll be out of the city within the hour. Trust me when I tell you, they won't find me. But that's not what I want. When you hired me, you promised me a chance to win. A chance to sink my teeth into something worth killing. We know we're close. You can walk away now, or you can be a hero and get your hands dirty."

Maggie glanced through the window toward Dan, then back to Coulier.

"What about Dan? He's going to talk. You have to know that."

"As governor, you could pardon him."

Maggie's head twitched. "For *what*?"

"For poisoning the harbor, of course."

Her heart skipped a beat. She tried to speak but didn't know what to say.

Coulier placed his hand on top of hers. "The evidence is already planted, Maggie. Don't let your love for a weak man prevent you from being the hero the people deserve."

# 25

**Corinth, Mississippi**

The dingy bulbs spilling light over the abandoned parking lot flickered. Clouds filled the sky, blocking out any glow from the moon and leaving the small Mississippi town in alternating patches of dull yellow and total darkness. It wasn't as cold as it had been in Kansas or the mountains, and Reed relaxed with the window down, enjoying a soft, humid breeze. A cigarette dangled from his fingers, its ember emitting a drifting trail of grey between puffs.

*God, the nicotine tastes good.*

From the passenger seat, Banks examined the abandoned shopping strip across the street. All the windows were boarded up. Stray trash drifted across the concrete, and a couple cats scampered amongst the shadows. But there were no people. No shopping carts full of groceries pushed by harried mothers dragging whining toddlers back to the smelly confines of unwashed minivans.

"It was a Food World," Banks said suddenly.

Reed took a long pull of the cigarette and regarded the outline of the old logo on the face of the store. The sign itself was long gone now, but the shadow remained.

"They used to be all over Mississippi," Banks continued. "They were owned by Bruno's, I think."

Reed nodded slowly, still staring at the outline of the logo. "I remember."

"I wonder what happened to them."

"The Food Worlds? They went bankrupt. Smothered by the big guys, I guess. Just couldn't compete."

Banks snorted a soft, humorless laugh. "That's life, isn't it? Small things getting smothered."

Reed wasn't sure what to say to that, so he just held the cigarette between his teeth while watching the cats chase a stray paper bag.

"How long have you smoked?"

Reed sucked out the last of the nicotine, then flicked the butt into the parking lot. He shrugged. "Since high school, I guess. Wasn't really a habit until Iraq."

"It's not good for you," she murmured.

"Neither is being shot at."

"You think that guy will come back? The one who shot at us in North Carolina and Nashville?"

Reed pondered the question a moment, his mind drifting back to Wolfgang, the brutal assassin that Salvador had hired to hunt him down. Wolfgang was an odd fish; he didn't work with Oliver's company, and Reed had never encountered him before. Granted, Wolfgang was both better trained and more intelligent than the two goons who tried to wreck them at the fuel station earlier that day, but Reed wasn't really concerned about the man they called The Wolf.

"I don't think so," he said at last. "He's got no skin in the game, and the man who was paying him is . . . no longer with us."

Banks was there when Wolfgang gunned down the South American gangster who hired him just a few miles west of Nashville. Reed didn't need to remind her about it.

"What about the guys today?" she asked.

"They're dead."

"I'm aware. Are there more of them?"

Reed had hoped Banks wouldn't ask that question. He'd danced around it all afternoon long. "They worked for my old boss. The British guy you shot in North Carolina."

"The bald prick."

Reed snorted. "Yeah . . . the bald prick."

"Did he send them after us *before* I shot him?"

Reed slid another cigarette out of his pocket but didn't light it. He twisted it between his lips, pondering the question in his tired mind. Banks had cut right to the heart of the problem—the same problem he'd been working through on the long drive to Mississippi. If Oliver was dead prior to Cowboy and Zeus being dispatched, then somebody else must have hired them. Of course, Reed had considered the possibility that the two contract killers hunted him down out of a simple desire for vengeance over their dead boss, but that wasn't likely. There was no love lost between Oliver and his contractors, and nobody who worked for the old killer would risk their own neck against one of their colleagues unless they were being paid. *Well paid.*

And that brought to mind Cowboy's fleeting comment, right before Reed sent two slugs crashing through his face: *"Two million is two million."*

Who would have paid Zeus and Cowboy two million dollars to bring down The Prosecutor? And if this individual offered the job to Zeus and Cowboy, had they also offered it to the remainder of Oliver's displaced, unemployed killers?

"Reed?" Banks looked toward him.

He realized he'd drifted off. "Yeah?"

"Are they coming?"

Her eyes were clear, without a trace of fear or trepidation, but there was no light in them. No fire or joy. None of the brilliant colors that stole his heart the moment she stepped on stage in Atlanta.

"I don't know," he said. It was an honest answer, but not a complete one. The complete answer would've been, *"I don't know, but probably so."*

Reed checked his watch and lit the cigarette. It was closing in on nine p.m., and still the parking lot lay empty. The quiet two-lane highway that passed in front of the abandoned shopping strip featured only an occasional car, but any one of those occasional cars could wind up being a bored cop who decided to check out the unknown sedan parked in the shadows. They couldn't afford to be discovered.

"How do you know this guy?"

Reed glanced toward Banks, sucked on the smoke a moment, then shrugged. "Business associate."

"You seem to have a lot of those."

Reed smirked. "Stay alive, and you will, too."

Banks sighed dramatically and reached for the door. Before she could lift the latch, a dull thumping sound drifted through the air, coming from the highway. Reed grabbed her hand and pulled her low, reaching for Cowboy's backup gun. The thumping sound grew louder, now the distinct bass tone of an oversized stereo. A moment later, the beat was joined by the hum of tires, and then a vehicle broke around the corner, careening toward the parking lot. It was an old Chevrolet panel van, painted a high-gloss green with murals of naked Greek gods on the sides. The windows were tinted pitch black, and the vehicle bounced over potholes and worn-down speedbumps like a dune buggy, crashing directly toward the sedan.

Reed muttered a low curse and sat up, throwing the door open. The van slid to a stop, sending loose gravel spraying across the lot as the music continued to blast—pounding bass mixed with screaming Spanish rap. Reed banged the butt of the handgun against the passenger's glass and shouted through the door.

"Shut that off! Are you out of your mind?"

The music died with the van's engine, and the parking lot was blanketed in silence again. Reed shot a paranoid glance back at the highway, but no other cars appeared around the corner. The lights flickered overhead, and the van remained still. Reed turned to tell Banks to stay in the car, but she was already out, her hands jammed into her pockets as she approached the van, one eyebrow raised. Reed sighed and holstered the gun.

The driver's side door of the van swung open with a creak, and two boots smacked the concrete. A clownishly short Hispanic man rounded the front of the van, his lips spread into a wide grin. "Prosecutor, baby. How are you?" He spoke with a heavy Mexican accent, his voice a great deal louder than was necessary.

Before Reed could stop him, the Mexican threw himself forward and wrapped the big American in a hug, his leather jacket squeaking against Reed's dirty clothes.

"*Pinche,* bruh! You smell like an ashtray. What's wrong with you?" The Mexican recoiled, wrinkling his nose over his olive lips.

"I've told you about the hugging," Reed said. "I don't like it."

The Mexican laughed and smacked Reed with the back of his hand. "When you call T-Rex, you get the T-Rex hug, baby. You know me. I . . . oh, mama. Who do we have here?"

Before Reed could stop him, T-Rex circled around Reed and made a beeline for Banks, his grin widening as he approached her.

"Oh, baby, you getting the *chingar* on, eh? Who da señorita?"

Reed moved to intercept him, but it was too late. T-Rex wrapped Banks in an aggressive hug and planted an even more enthusiastic kiss right on her mouth. Banks choked and blinked, too shocked to resist.

T-Rex followed up the kiss with a gentle smack on her butt, and then a wink. "*¿Reed comparte?*"

Banks's hand flashed like a striking rattlesnake, cracking across T-Rex's face before Reed could stop her. "*¡Chinga tu madre!*"

The parking lot fell silent, and Reed snapped his mouth shut, unaware that it had fallen open.

T-Rex touched his cheek. It blazed red, with clear white marks left by Banks's fingers. He broke into a gentle laugh. "Daaamn, bro. You wanna bring my *mama* into this?" The laugh grew louder until he bent over, still rubbing his inflamed cheek.

Reed shot Banks a confused glance, and she shrugged. A small smile played at the corner of her lips.

He decided it was time to take control again, and he pushed forward, smacking T-Rex on the arm. "Rex. Stop screwing around. You came roaring in here like a bat out of hell. There could've been an army of cops on your ass!"

The Mexican continued to laugh, shaking his head and gesturing toward Banks. "Dawg, your lady *cold,* bro. I'm sayin' she *cold*!"

He held his side and disappeared around to the back of the van.

Reed tilted his head to one side. "What did he say?"

Banks scoffed. "Something outrageous."

"I didn't know you spoke Spanish."

She shot him a saucy smirk before walking after T-Rex. "There's a lot you don't know."

Reed pushed his hands into his pockets, unable to tear his eyes away from her hips as the quiet confidence returned to her stride. He could watch that swagger all night long.

Banks disappeared behind the van, and Reed hurried after her. T-Rex had already opened both doors and was busy unloading cans of paint onto the concrete.

"She smacks like a *puta*, baby."

"*Chinga tu madre*," Banks hissed again.

T-Rex broke into a big grin. "Again with my mama? Baby, you so cold. But you know what? My mama *is* a *puta*, so I'm not getting spicy over it." He chuckled and set the last of the paint on the concrete, then reached for the wooden cabinet that filled the back of the van. He paused a moment and shot Reed a sideways look. "She cool for real though, right?"

Reed sighed and made a get-on-with-it motion.

"All right. If you say so. Let's see what we got."

T-Rex pressed his hand against the wooden panel, and it snapped open, falling flat on hinges against the bottom of the van and exposing a wide wooden drawer behind it. T-Rex grabbed the rope handle of the drawer and dragged it outward on smooth metal rails. As wide as the van and at least eight feet deep, the drawer rolled into the flashing light of the overhead bulbs, and Reed heard a soft gasp escape Banks's lips.

The drawer was packed to the brim with firearms—handguns, assault rifles, shotguns, backpack mortars, and sniper rifles. Lines of every model, caliber, and variation were crammed in alongside cases of ammunition, stacks of optics, and enough magazines to lay down a small army. Near the back of the drawer, the firearms were joined by packages of C4, hand grenades, flashbangs, and knives. In all, there were well over a hundred different weapons, all neatly packed between soft foam partitions, but that wasn't all. Hanging from a rack near the driver's seat, lines of body armor, jumpsuits, and stacks of combat boots filled the front of the van. Everything an operator would need to go to war.

T-Rex grinned and turned toward Banks. He shoved his elbows into his sides and wiggled his hands as though they were suspended at the end of six-inch arms. “T-Rex, baby. *Small arms dealer*.”

Confusion clouded Banks’s face, no doubt exacerbated by the grandiose display of firepower spread out before her, then she broke into a laugh that was soon joined by T-Rex. They stared at the drawer and indulged in delirious chuckles, smacking each other on the shoulder while Reed stood awkwardly by, wondering what the hell was happening.

Banks jabbed a finger toward T-Rex. “I got that one. That’s good, man.”

T-Rex shrugged, his reddened cheek flushing a shade darker. “Hey, baby. I do what I can, you know? Gotta keep the laughs rolling with fools like him around.”

Reed pushed forward, hovering over the drawer. “All right, dude. You’ve had your laugh. We’re on a tight schedule.”

“I got you, baby. I got you. What kind of job we running?”

Reed scanned the lines of firearms, then pulled another cigarette from his pocket. “Let’s just say you’ll catch the details on CNN.”

The grin widened across the arms dealer’s face. “Say no more.”

# 26

**Upstate New York**

Wolfgang's eyes stung. He squinted at the complex image on the computer screen, his right hand gently adjusting the focus of the digital microscope next to the computer. The contents of the glass slide pinned beneath the microscope were clear as water to the naked eye. But beneath superhuman magnification of the multi-thousand-dollar tool, the dynamic contents of the solution were exposed in radical detail. Wolfgang peered through protective goggles and adjusted the microscope again, tracing the clean outlines of DNA structure across the screen with the tip of a pen.

The gentle rise and fall of his chest ceased completely as his focus reached subconscious levels, dominating his body. This skillset was both priceless and destructive—the ability to become so engrossed in his work that nothing around him mattered anymore. Days could pass, and he wouldn't remember to eat or sleep. Nothing but work.

Wolfgang adjusted the brightness of the screen and continued to trace the DNA outline, searching each base pair. It was human DNA, but not healthy DNA. He could discern the disjointed patterns, the irregular breaks in proper DNA code. All telltale signs of a major genetic disorder. This was his control slide—the DNA in its natural form prior to being subjected to treatment. The next slide would tell the truth.

Pausing to scratch notes onto a cluttered pad, Wolfgang swapped the slide out with a fresh one and drew a long, deep breath.

"This time . . ." he whispered, then focused on the DNA construction. "No . . ." The ragged word slipped through his lips, half-plea, half-objection. He adjusted the zoom, increased the brightness, and peered again, squinting, insisting that the pattern would change, that this string of complex human encoding would somehow be different from the last.

But it wasn't. The DNA looked identical to the previous set, unaffected by ten weeks of steady, rigorous treatment.

Wolfgang screamed and slammed his hand into the desk, sending the notepad flying. The underground laboratory thundered with his repeated shouts as glass slides rocketed off the metal table and spun onto the floor, bursting into pieces. He crashed against a swivel stool, slinging the goggles onto the floor amid the mess. He rested his face in his hands, his shoulders rising and falling in ragged sobs.

*Six years.*

For six years, Wolfgang stared at that screen, manipulated slides, and tweaked DNA, working with every known formula he could get his hands on—any type of medicated substance that could influence the broken patterns of each base pair. But this time, he thought he was onto something. Early tests indicated that this formula could produce the results he was looking for. And yet, six months, four hundred thousand dollars, and countless sleepless nights later . . . nothing. Not a trace of progress.

He lifted his head and scanned the laboratory around him. Across the room, a counter lined with more microscopes and several thousand dollars' worth of top-shelf scientific equipment stood beneath clinical cabinets packed with the same. Next to the counter, two built-in refrigerators with glass doors glowed in a soft LED light, packed with samples, Petri dishes, and every formula or chemical he possessed that required refrigeration.

And then the metal table, stretching the middle of the room, stacked with his most expensive research equipment. Two hundred thousand dollars' worth of the very best medical computers money could buy. The brain of his entire project, humming almost silently beneath the table while sending the visual results of its work to the dozen-odd screens lining the table.

*Worthless.*

Wolfgang got up and stumbled across the room, opening a bolted steel door that led to a narrow stairway. Past two more locked and sealed doors, he kicked off his rubber shoes and stepped into the dark confines of his ground-level living room.

In the darkness of tall hardwoods, the house was nestled a mile off the road and far from the casual glance of anyone. Amid the shade of the trees, with no exterior lights or interior TV screens, the home rested in almost perfect darkness.

Wolfgang settled into a leather chair. His head, neck, and back all ached as if he'd been hit by a car, but the quiet of the home was reassuring, providing minor relief to his strained nerves. Wolfgang felt safe there, seated in a windowless room, miles from civilization, alone in the dark. He didn't have to worry about the dozens of shady characters around the world who knew him as The Wolf, a practiced, deadly killer. He didn't have to think about his next job, or for that matter, his last job. He could push the violence out of his mind and focus on what really mattered to him—the only thing that mattered to him.

*Collins.*

He lifted a worn, leather-bound photo album from an end table and flipped it open. It was really too dark in the living room to clearly see each image, but it didn't matter. He had every shot memorized. Every detail. Every smile.

Collins, at her first birthday party, seated at the end of the cheap card table inside the single-wide trailer, their mother bent over next to her, smiling. Collins's twisted, pained face was flushed red, but there was a smile on her lips as she stared down at the tiny birthday cake set before her. There was no one else in the room—just their mother, Wolfgang, and her.

He flipped a few pages, moving past pained memories of their impoverished childhood buried in the Appalachian Mountains of West Virginia. Collins was older now, fifteen, smiling as she stood next to her pony. Wolfgang bought the animal in Scotland and had it shipped to a horse farm in Pennsylvania, where Collins would visit it when she felt up to leaving her facility. These days, that was less and less often, as the dreaded clutches of her disease dug deeper into her fragile body.

They called it cystic fibrosis, a brutal genetic disorder that wrecked Collins's entire life. It started in her lungs, filling them with putrid mucus that made every breath agony and took over from there. She didn't gain weight and rarely experienced any surplus of energy. Wheezing and persistent coughing ruled her days and kept her awake late into the night. Even with the assistance of an oxygen bottle, her lungs struggled to keep up with her body's demands. She once described it to Wolfgang as what she imagined astronauts felt as they stared at Earth from outer space—breathless.

Collins loved the sky. She loved the stars, and astronomy, and all things NASA. With her quick wit and sharp mind, Wolfgang had no doubt she could have become an astronaut had the curse of CF not destroyed her life. He hated the disease for that. Hated it not for the pain it inflicted, but for the life it stole. All life—even the best lives—experienced pain. It was a natural part of the human experience. But CF stole the *experience*, limiting Collins on where she could live, what sorts of activities and hobbies she could attempt, and even the people who were willing to share a life with her.

*That* was the worst part. The loneliness. Wolfgang knew what that loneliness felt like because he subjected himself to it on a daily basis, locking himself away in the confines of his subterranean laboratory for weeks on end, only surfacing to earn enough money to continue his research. Sure, there had been spells where he studied in Scotland or took a driving tour of Europe, moments when he couldn't go on any further, and he just needed to be selfish.

But over the past couple years, those moments became further and further apart. The mask he wore around other people—the quippy, intelligent, almost jovial face of a happy-go-lucky killer—felt thin lately, ready to break, as though at some point, he would expose himself to the outside world.

He didn't care about that. He didn't care about anything outside of Collins. The work he did, gory though it was, seemed a small price to pay for her eventual health. The bad people he killed didn't deserve to consume the precious oxygen Collins so desperately needed. Wolfgang made peace with bashing their skulls in and being paid to do it. What bothered him about the cracking mask wasn't his own personal jeopardy—it was the possibility that he may not finish his work. His *magnum opus*—the calling of his life.

Wolfgang closed the book. He never watched the TV in his room, but he spent a great deal of time staring at the wall above it where a wide canvas painting hung, brutally simple in its construct, with a white background and simple black letters painted in elegant calligraphy: *ER-004*.

He sighed. ER-004, the silver bullet he so longed to capture. It was four years before that Wolfgang stumbled into the research team that eventually developed ER-004, a pre-birth treatment plan for a disease called *X-Linked hypohidrotic ectodermal dysplasia*. Even with a mind that naturally grasped medical concepts, it took Wolfgang time to memorize the disease, but it took only moments to understand what it meant. It was a brutal, genetic disorder that affected people's ability to sweat while wreaking havoc on their skin. Up until the development of ER-004, XLHED could be identified prior to birth, but there was little to be done other than manage it with whatever insufficient drugs could be applied.

That research team changed everything, though. They discovered a protein replacement therapy, which, prior to birth, demonstrated the ability to stop the catastrophic effects of XLHED. The therapy stalled after phase one of clinical trials but still showed promising signs of progressing into a real, life-changing treatment. Even a cure, maybe.

After discovering the work being conducted on ER-004, Wolfgang's life erupted into hope. If a method could be manufactured to treat XLHED, why not a method to treat CF? Maybe even reverse it? They weren't all that different in nature; they were both genetic and could be attacked with protein replacement therapy, at least in theory. It was at that moment that what was once a part-time pipe-dream pursuit to find a cure for Collins became a consuming obsession. His entire life was swallowed into the hunt for a cure.

Wolfgang continued staring at the painting, thinking about his numerous conversations with every scientist on the project who would speak to him. On nights like this, when despair clouded out the tiniest rays of hope, he would stare at the painting and remind himself that it *was* possible. It had to be.

Wolfgang sighed and pushed himself to his feet, leaving the album on the table beside him. It was much past his usual bedtime—if he really had such a thing. Tomorrow he needed to drive to Buffalo to refit for a new job. This one would take him out of the country for a couple weeks, to the Middle East, probably. Most of his high-paying jobs took him to the Middle East these days.

Around the hall and to the stairs, he placed one foot on the bottom step and reached for the banister before he felt the dull buzz on his hip. Wolfgang froze, then pulled his phone from its belt holster. He squinted at the backlit screen.

PERIMETER ALERT. INTRUDER, ZONE 1.

A rush of adrenaline pumped into his blood as he drew the Walther 9mm from his ankle. He retraced his steps back into the living room, then through the kitchen, toward the front door. The alarm panel blinked reassuringly on the wall, indicating that whatever disturbance had triggered the alert was probably just a fallen limb or a stray animal. Wolfgang placed his finger on the trigger and crouched low below the windows, five feet from the front door. He navigated to the surveillance app on his phone, and a few taps later produced night-vision-assisted views of the entire front of his house. Each camera displayed empty, cleared screens. Nothing but trees, the drive, and . . .

Wolfgang zoomed in on the ninth camera angle, focusing on the front porch. A foreign object lay next to the door, appearing to be a small yellow package, about the size of a postcard. Even with the state-of-the-art camera system, it was difficult to determine much more than that, but the object definitely wasn't there when he locked the door two days prior.

With a quick flip of the lock, he slipped the front door open, clearing the porch and the surrounding yard before glancing toward his feet. Sure enough, the package leaned against the wall with a simple black script written across its face.

*For The Wolf.*

Wolfgang hesitated a moment, then prodded the package with his foot. It fell over without a sound, and he wondered if it was empty. It was thin and light. A bomb? Poison? He'd never seen either weapon packaged in such a slim parcel.

After scooping the envelope up, he retreated back into the house and locked the door, then trotted into the kitchen. He set the gun down on the counter and examined the envelope from each side. No traces of suspicious substances caught his eye. The envelope wasn't even sealed. Wolfgang tipped it up and shook it gently until a small white card, blank on one side, and a glass vial, no bigger than a large pill, spilled onto the counter.

He held the vial up to the light, squinting through the clear plastic. Some type of water-like formula was housed inside, sealed by a tight plug. He set the vial down, then flipped the card over. A short message was scrawled on the back, and the words froze the breath in his throat.

*Found what you're looking for. RM has the rest.*

# 27

**Port of Mobile**
**Mobile, Alabama**

Gambit stood next to the dock and watched from two hundred yards away as crowds of migrant workers unloaded the *Santa Coquina.* Nestled close to the edge of the port, with her bow buried in darkness and just enough lights to get the job done, the priceless load of banana crates was being lifted out of the hold of the old reefer, then loaded onto three semitrucks. Each truck was equipped with a crew of team drivers, ready to hit the highway as soon as the goods were packed. While the trailers themselves were all unmarked, small DOT inscriptions were printed on the truck's doors.

HOLIDAY LOGISTICS COMPANY
BRUNSWICK, GA

Gambit lowered the binoculars and took a long sip of hot coffee. Standing this close to the water's edge, even so far south, the wind chilled him to the bone. It would take another four hours to unload the *Santa Coquina,* maybe five, and he would watch every moment of it.

But for now, there was another job to do. Gambit's stomach tightened at the thought. No matter how many times he made this call, how many times he proved himself to be his boss's most valuable asset, Gambit still felt the edge of a knife beneath his every step, as though at any moment, with the slightest slip, he could fall and be split in half.

It wasn't paranoia. Gambit was there when Aiden's previous second-in-command met his doom for failing to deliver. Gambit was there because, at the time, Gambit was third-in-command. Pressing that trigger and watching Number 2 collapse to the concrete ushered him a little closer to Aiden's side, and conversely, a little closer to his own death.

Gambit pressed the call button and held the phone to his ear. Maybe Aiden wouldn't answer. Maybe this conversation could wait. No such luck.

Aiden answered on the third ring. "Yes?"

"The ship made port. Unloading now. The trucks will be on the road before sunrise."

"Is that sufficient?"

"I think so. Illinois and New York won't be a problem. California is questionable."

"Make sure the drivers understand what's at stake." Aiden's words were calm and cold, betraying none of the fire and fury he was capable of.

Gambit swallowed. All day he had debated whether to disclose the incident with the Coast Guard. The *Santa Coquina*'s captain, Jose Cortez, had assured him that the Coast Guard was only making a routine "inspection," but nothing about the boarding felt routine to Gambit. Fourteen men, all armed, taking control of the ship at a moment's notice? He knew the Coast Guard performed random boardings, but it seemed unlikely that they would employ this much force unless they were tipped off.

"Anything else?" Aiden's voice was dry.

Gambit couldn't be sure if Aiden already knew about the boarding or not but assuming he did, failing to disclose it could be fatal.

"Yes. The *Santa Coquina* was boarded yesterday by the Coast Guard."

Aiden didn't respond. Did he already know, or was he simply processing the information?

"They didn't find anything," Gambit said. "Captain Cortez assures me it was a routine inspection."

Another moment of silence.

Gambit's fingers went numb. Every natural instinct commanded him to keep talking, keep providing irrelevant details to fill the deathly stillness until his boss spoke, but he didn't. Aiden didn't appreciate meaningless chatter.

"What do you think?" Aiden said at last.

It wasn't the question Gambit expected. He hesitated, then decided to stick to his policy of honesty. "They boarded in force. Fourteen armed men from some type of speedboat. I don't think it was routine."

Again, further explanations and comments swelled at the edge of Gambit's consciousness, but he waited.

"It was the emergency entry filings," Aiden said. "The shipping company filed too many, too quickly."

Gambit agreed but didn't feel the need to say so.

"See to it that Captain Cortez and the *Santa Coquina* become a statistic on the return voyage. It's unlikely that he's suspicious, but the last thing we need is a curious shipping crew poking their nose around my cargo. Once this shipment is off the trucks, we'll terminate our contract with the shipping company and find a new boat and crew."

Gambit took a sip of coffee, then cleared his throat. "What about Governor Trousdale?"

"What about her?"

"She may have ordered the boarding. I recommend we put her on ice as soon as possible."

Aiden grunted. "Agreed. Where are we with Montgomery?"

"Two of Oliver Enfield's men made a pass at him in Kansas yesterday. They're both dead, but it looked bloody. At least one of them came pretty close."

"Are any of the other contractors on his trail?"

"It's impossible to be sure. Maybe. Montgomery also had a run-in with the FBI in Cheyenne."

"The FBI? Is that right?"

"I'm not sure how, but they've identified him. He's on their Most Wanted List."

"Excellent. That could be very helpful. Where is he now?"

"The best I can tell . . . closing in on Alabama."

Gambit waited to see if Aiden would reach the same conclusion he had.

A low, sinister chuckle erupted through the speaker. "Oh, he's going to find Daddy, isn't he? Couldn't get what he needed from Carter, so now he's going after his old man."

"I thought so."

"He's playing right into our hand. Do you think he's worn down enough to be useful?"

Gambit bit his lip. He'd been asking himself the same question all day. There was no clear answer. "If he's not, it'll be easy enough to leave him in a ditch and find another way to address Trousdale."

"I agree. Get up to Alabama and take care of it, but be careful. He's very intelligent. Maybe even as intelligent as you. Don't give him too many clues."

"I understand."

The call ended, and Gambit lifted the binoculars, surveying the dockside crew. He swept his gaze to the rear of the ship and settled the binoculars just below the aft deck.

There. Right above the rudder. He could place a crude charge that would rupture the hull and flood the cargo bay. He would have the radios and all emergency devices disabled ahead of time. Nobody would ever know what happened. The *Santa Coquina* would simply vanish, never to be found again.

Meanwhile, Gambit would head north into the heart of Alabama, set a little trap, and make a couple more things vanish amid the smoke while he held the mirrors.

A couple things—or a couple people. Both named Montgomery.

# 28

**Jasper, Alabama**

Another small town, another dusty hotel room. Reed stared through a narrow opening in the curtains at the outdoor pool in the courtyard. The water was murky grey, with chunks of ice floating on the surface. He wondered why the staff hadn't pumped it dry prior to the winter season, and then he wondered why it was ever full of water at all. This didn't feel like the sort of place that would make time or money for a pool. The room was only forty bucks a night.

For a moment he imagined the water wasn't grey, but bright blue, without any ice, and with a hot sun beating down from overhead. Next to the pool, a Rally Green Camaro with white racing stripes glistened in the sun. A small boy played in the water, splashing and screaming, while his mother, ignoring the boy, sunned herself in a lounge chair. She ignored him a lot, probably, and was more interested in the latest soap opera or lunch downtown with her friends.

A man in swim trunks stepped through the gate and onto the pool deck. He screamed and leapt into the deep end with all the enthusiasm of his six-year-old son. A giant splash erupted over the deck, and the woman caught the edge of it. She squealed, then cursed at the man, but he ignored her, now wrestling with his son. They dunked each other, screaming and thrashing about, with little or no care for the other guests or the woman. Their smiles, cries, gestures . . . so much happiness. So much peace.

Reed pushed the vision back into the dusty caverns of his memory.

*It hurts too much.*

The bathroom door clicked behind him, and he turned to see Banks step out, wrapped in a towel. Her hair was wet trailing her shoulders, and sending fresh water droplets streaming down her back as she walked to the bed and sat down on the edge. Next to her, spread out over the comforter, was everything Reed acquired from T-Rex. Everything he would need to breach the prison: weapons, gear, two burner phones, and a flashlight.

Reed ran his hand over his face, then walked to the bathroom sink. He peeled his smelly shirt off and ran cool water over his face and through his hair. The touch of water eased his tension, if only a little.

*So long ago. And yet it feels like yesterday.*

"What are you thinking about?"

Banks's soft voice broke the stillness, and Reed straightened. His back crackled, bringing moderate relief to the ache of two days of solid driving. He toweled off his face and leaned against the counter, facing Banks again. "Just about tonight. What I have to do. How I'm going to do it."

Banks nodded softly, picking at a loose thread in the towel. "What am I going to do?"

Reed had been waiting for that question. He walked across the room, picked up a SIG 9mm handgun from the nightstand and began to feed hollow-point rounds into the magazine, one at a time.

"We're going to approach the prison from the northeast. There's an old dirt road there, next to the forest. You'll wait in the car while I go get him."

"You know the prison that well?"

Reed shrugged. "I've never been there, if that's what you're asking."

"So what makes you think you can just . . . *go get him*?"

Another good question Reed wasn't entirely ready to answer.

"I have some experience with prisons. I secured the blueprints from an associate earlier today and reviewed them. I know where the psych ward is. My basic plan is to move fast and make noise. These places are designed to keep people in, not out. It's a pretty old facility, also, and it's medium security. I doubt there'll be many challenges."

Reed paused over the magazine a moment, a bullet held between his fingers. "I feel like this is useless to say, but you should walk away. I know you don't trust me anymore, but I promise you, I will follow this mess to its core, and I will deal with the man who killed your father. At this point, you're only associating yourself with a series of events that will almost certainly destroy your life. I don't want that for you."

Banks continued to trace her knee, staring at the floor. "I trust you," she whispered.

Reed's fingers felt suddenly numb. The bullet slipped out of his hand, tumbling over the matted carpet. She held his gaze, her face so full of pain that he wanted nothing more than to look away. And yet he couldn't. It wasn't possible.

"Then you should go," he said softly. "Get away from all of this. Let me finish it alone."

"I don't think you realize," she said. "You and I aren't so different. I don't have anyplace to go. Anything to do. The only thing getting me out of bed in the morning is the idea that somewhere, at the end of this tunnel, there is a man I can hold responsible for it all. I realize I'm not that useful, tactically speaking, but I'm going with you. I'm going to deal with this myself."

It was the answer he expected, albeit a lot more articulate and calm. Even so, her confidence made it no easier to walk ahead, carrying her with him into this fire.

Reed lifted a burner phone off the bed and passed it to her. The phone, along with its identical mate, the handgun, and a slew of other gear, was secured from T-Rex.

"I'll have the other one," Reed said. "My number is the only one programmed inside. If something goes wrong, lose the phone. You don't want the police to find it."

She nodded once, then walked back into the bathroom, closing the door a moment. When she emerged, she wore jeans and a T-shirt, and her hair was pulled into a loose ponytail.

*Damn, she looks good.*

Reed stared until she noticed.

She brushed bangs out of her face and shrugged. "What?"

Reed hesitated, feeling confused, and very tired.

*Now isn't the time. But will there ever be another chance?*

He walked across the room, gently lifted one hand, and touched her elbow. She flinched a little and crossed her arms, but she didn't back away.

"Banks . . ." He whispered her name, although he wasn't sure why.

She looked toward the floor, and again the lump welled in his throat, blocking every good intention.

*Now or never.*

"Banks, I know I've hurt you. I know I've dragged you through hell, and none of this is your fault. You are a beautiful, amazing person. You're . . . unlike any person I've ever known. The night I first met you, I should've told you that. I was too stunned to say, but . . . I—"

"Stop."

The single word shut him down as if a bullet had struck his brain. Her tone broke, and tears flowed down her cheeks. When she looked up, her bright blue eyes were flooded with pain, anger, confusion, and other twisted agonies he couldn't begin to untangle.

"Don't say it," she whispered. "Don't you ever say it. I believed in you, Reed. Even after Atlanta. Even after you ran me off the road in my own car and we ran for our lives from a madman chunking grenades at us, *I believed in you*. Because I always believe there's a reason or a good thing behind it all. But you know what? Sometimes there's not. Sometimes life is just messed up. And I don't think you know what you're saying, so don't say it. Don't you hurt me. I'm done hurting."

She walked into the bathroom and closed the door, leaving Reed standing alone next to the sink, staring back at himself in a dirty mirror.

# 29

**Winston County, Alabama**

The swaying tips of leafless limbs overhung the forest floor, splitting the light of the moon into a thousand dancing shards. A cool mist hung just above the ground, suspended by the rapidly changing weather. Reed wasn't sure what sort of storm was blowing up from the west, but he could see the cloud bank headed toward him, beyond the trees and over the next ridge.

There were secrets in these trees. Reed knew some of them—ancient tales of treachery and betrayal dating back to the American Civil War when Winston County declared its independence from the Confederacy and was thereafter known as *the Free State of Winston.* In those years, these woods were home to scavengers and thieves, the refuse of war who pillaged the towns and raped their way through communities far and wide. As law returned to the land over the coming decades, Winston County became a refuge for other sorts of rejects—moonshiners and petty criminals, the bottom of the barrel in a poor, broken state.

David Montgomery loved to tell Reed the stories of these hills, situated northwest of their hometown of Birmingham. Most of them were probably tall tales at best, but even now, a lifetime of bloodshed and violence away from his childhood, the old stories returned. Standing four hundred yards from the prison, Reed wondered if David ever recalled the old tales, if they kept him up at night as his tired, shattered mind screamed for peace in a lonely prison cell. Did David retain that much identity? That much memory?

Reed paused behind a red oak and wiped his runny nose with the back of a gloved hand. It wasn't the legends of lynchings and hooded men that chilled him to the bone, nor was it the cold wind that blew down from the mountains. It was another thought—one much more personal and painful than any haunted story. The thought that David Montgomery, now a shell of a man, may not recognize his own son.

Reed gritted his teeth and checked the handgun strapped to his side—the SIG 9mm loaded with hollow-points. Over his back he wore a pump-action shotgun loaded with rubber bullets, which rode on top of a vest packed with bulletproof plates. Strapped to that vest were half a dozen flashbang grenades. Black boots, black pants, and a black baseball cap completed the ensemble, making him look like the ghost of a spec ops soldier.

He wasn't here to kill anyone—even the guards who may well try to kill him. The flashbangs and the rubber bullets in the shotgun would help protect him without causing any lasting damage to their victims. The handgun would be a last resort, long after all nonlethal methods of reaching David failed.

Reed crouched to the forest floor, creeping toward the fence line that loomed up out of the mist. The fence was maybe twelve feet, with razor wire curled along its top. Impending though it was, there were no guard towers situated around the perimeter of the prison, and no correctional officers leading German shepherds pacing next to the fence. This wasn't that kind of prison. It was nothing like the maximum-security fortress Reed once called home back in Colorado.

Even so, Reed was well aware that there would be roadblocks. He could cut through the fence and slip up on the main dormitory of the prison—a two-story block building with steel doors. Other than the single guard tower at the main gate, correctional officers outside the dormitory were unlikely.

Behind the primary block building, there was an open yard with tennis nets, basketball hoops, and some minor exercise equipment—standard stuff for a medium-security prison. Beyond the yard, another block building stood by itself, a little smaller than the first, but still two-level. Unlike the first, this building featured only narrow windows and one entrance, guarded by a lone yellow lamp. The psych ward.

Other than a garage full of institution vehicles and a dormant garden spot situated next to the psych ward, that was all the prison consisted of. It was simple and utilitarian, built by the tax-weary people of Alabama.

Reed knelt next to the fence and pulled wire cutters from his cargo pocket. They were really too small for this gauge of wire and took considerable force to complete the cut, but they were the best T-Rex could produce on short notice.

A few minutes of muted snaps resulted in a hole big enough for Reed to worm through. He pushed the shotgun ahead of him, then followed up with as little noise as he could manage. He crouched in the darkness for a full minute, listening for any sign that he had been detected, but there was nothing. The prison lay as silent as it had an hour before.

A few careful minutes of negotiating the shadows led him behind the main prison block and another hundred yards to the far edge of the yard. Once there, he descended to his stomach and wormed his way toward the psych ward, still hugging the shadows and keeping constant surveillance of each corner of the prison. The wide, double doors of the ward were tall and windowless, like the rest of the building. Flowerbeds circled the entrance but lay barren in the cold. Reed could detect at least one security camera mounted at the top corner of the building, but he was confident his position was outside the camera's view. Seventy yards away at the entrance of the prison, he made out the ball-capped head of a security guard sitting inside the guard shack with a book held at eye level. Certainly, there would be other officers inside the prison, and they would be armed, but until he breached the door, they wouldn't become threats.

*What now?*

Reed lay in the darkness, peering at the door to the psych ward. He knew from the blueprints that a reception area was on the other side—a desk with bulletproof glass, a guard, and a locked door that led into the core of the ward. Unlike the main prison block behind him, the psych ward wasn't organized into large dormitories with rows of bunk beds and inmates sharing a common room. It was subdivided into small cells, with regular steel doors, reinforced glass, and the same standard door bolts typically found in a hospital. The doors were designed more to keep the prisoners apart than out of fear of an escape attempt. These people were insane, after all, and it wasn't worth the risk of a fight.

Standard bolts though they were, Reed didn't have time to pick any locks. He needed the keys, which meant he needed to get behind the bulletproof glass. How he was going to do that, or how he was going to locate his father in potentially dozens of cells, were problems he would have to solve on the fly.

Reed pushed out the clutter of thoughts threatening to shatter his focus, and immediately, her face broke through the darkness, filling his mind—her eyes, so wide, so beautiful, and so full of pain. Pain that *he* caused.

No. He couldn't think about her right now. Couldn't think about the gut-wrenching things she had said to him or the way they made him want to eat a bullet. Banks, a mile away, was huddled in the stolen sedan, waiting for him to bring back the man who would help her find justice. That was all she cared about, and all he could afford to care about.

Reed wiped his nose, rose to a crouch, and checked the shotgun. It was chambered and ready to go. He cradled the weapon in one arm and took a cautious step toward the double doors of the ward.

The alarm was instantaneous, blaring out across the yard, filling every corner of the fenced prison with pounding waves of screeching noise. Reed jerked himself back into the shadows and pulled the shotgun into his shoulder, instantly regretting his decision to load it with rubber bullets. He ducked into the darkness, his hands turning white as he clamped his fingers around the weapon and searched the sky. Lights blazed from posts mounted at each corner of the prison, flooding the yard and fully exposing him while a yellow search beam swept back and forth from the lone guard tower.

Reed jumped up and dashed for the psych ward, pulling in close beneath the camera and praying like hell that he hadn't been seen.

*What the hell does that matter? I've already been seen. They're coming now.*

The siren continued. Shouts joined the mix, and Reed peered around the corner of the building, readying the shotgun and watching as correctional officers poured out of the main dormitory, shoving sleepy prisoners ahead of them.

A split second later, the twin doors blew back on their hinges, and two white-clothed COs rushed out, pushing a small crowd of stumbling prisoners with them.

And then it hit him. *It's not an intruder alarm. It's a fire alarm. What the hell happened?*

Reed didn't believe in luck. Not *that* much luck. He had some experience with tripping fire alarms in prisons, but that hadn't been his plan tonight. Was there actually a fire inside one of the dormitories? There was no way to know. The only option now was to take advantage.

Holding the shotgun into his shoulder, Reed pressed along the face of the ward, blending in with the crowd of bumbling psych prisoners almost instantly. He began searching the faces, tilting his head around shoulders and swinging arms, searching for any sign of the tall man with broad shoulders so similar to his own. Most of the men were much too short to be David.

Reed hurried past the crowd and dashed through the doors, still pushing amid a growing pileup of sleepy prisoners. He grabbed them one at a time, checking faces before reaching for the next.

"Hey! Who are you?"

A burly CO circled around from behind his desk, a nightstick swinging from one hand. Before he could approach, Reed launched himself through the crowd and drove a fist into the big man's face, knocking him back against the wall. He followed the blow with a knee to the stomach and a palm to the nose, sending his victim's skull cracking against the block wall. The CO crumpled to the ground, and Reed turned past him, rushing through another set of open doors and into the first hallway full of cells.

He didn't need to worry about keys or locked doors. Every cell door stood open, with a few straggling prisoners headed toward the door. A couple of them looked up, meeting his gaze as Reed plowed ahead, but nobody said anything. They all appeared doped up enough to walk in front of a train without noticing.

Fresh urgency poured into his mind as Reed fought his way through the last white-clad prisoners, checking each cell as he went. Empty room after empty room greeted him. The clamor of activity behind him grew quieter, but Reed knew there were more COs ahead. With only one entrance to the building—a major fire hazard, now that he thought about it—they would need to move all the prisoners off the second floor and down this hallway, giving him only seconds to finish his search.

One more cell on the left, then a cell on the right, and—

A crimson splash on the floor, just outside the last cell on the right, broke his thoughts. He pulled the shotgun into his shoulder and hurried forward, where two more blood drops stained the floor. Reed kicked the door open and shoved his way inside the cell, placing one finger on the trigger.

Reed's heart leapt into his throat, and he slowly lowered the gun. The cell was empty, featuring nothing save a bed and a small sink. But centered on the floor in a circle of red stains, was a die-cast car, the kind he found in cereal boxes as a kid.

And not just any car. A very particular, very specific car.

A Rally Green Camaro with white racing stripes.

# 30

**Winston County, Alabama**

Banks heard the scream of the fire alarm rip through the trees, and her heart sank. She threw open the door of the sedan and piled out, gripping a Smith & Wesson 9mm with one shaking hand as she stepped away from the wide dirt road and toward the alarm.

Did they find Reed already? Was this part of the plan? Reed hadn't mentioned any alarms or distractions. Indecision filled her crowded mind. Reed had said for her to run if something went wrong. "*Take the car, ditch the phone, and get as far away as possible before the sun comes up.*" But how could she know this wasn't part of the plan? How could she know Reed wouldn't be back minutes later, needing her and the car?

She dug the burner from her pocket and hit the power switch, her thumb hovering over the call button.

No. She couldn't call. What if this *were* part of the plan, and his phone rang? Surely he put it on silent. But if he didn't . . .

A snapping sound rang out from behind her. Banks gasped and whirled around, raising the handgun. Dark trees shrouded in mist hung close to the road, their ghostly limbs trailing near to the ground. She thought she saw a shadow pass between the trunks someplace beyond the ditch, but she couldn't be sure.

Banks swallowed and circled the car, keeping the gun up and her finger extended next to the trigger guard. Again, she thought she heard a dull crack, but this time it came from the other side of the road, back toward the prison. She began to turn again, already moving her finger into place over the trigger, but it was too late. A woman, dressed in all black, appeared out of nowhere, only two feet away. Her arms swung in smooth arcs, and then her hands closed around Banks's neck. Before she could scream, Banks felt herself being shoved off balance, pivoting on her own heels. Her face was sent careening toward the hard roof of the car. Banks tried to scream, but the roof collided with her nose, and everything went black.

---

Kelly caught the handgun as it slipped from Banks's limp hand. The blonde crumpled to the ground in a pitiful heap, and Kelly stepped over her, checking to be sure the pistol was chambered before she turned toward the alarms. She didn't relish bashing Reed's helpless girlfriend into the roof of a car or leaving her unconscious in the middle of a dirt road, but that was Reed's fault, not hers. He should have never brought an innocent woman into this mess.

*Another* innocent woman.

Kelly circled the car without glancing inside, then stepped through the ditch and started into the forest. Mist draped the spider-like limbs of the trees as she pressed closer to the sound of screaming sirens. Voices carried through the forest now—distant, but growing louder—and panicked shouts and orders snapped between whoops of the alarm.

It was exactly the kind of chaos Reed instigated wherever he went.

She stepped around a tree, pushed farther into the forest, and gripped the gun. It shook in her unsteady hand, and she stumbled over a log, just catching herself on a tree before falling into a ditch. Her stomach erupted in pain, sending shockwaves of agony up and down her torso and into her brain—the continued bite of the flames on her skin. The pain of the burns, the loss, and the hatred ruled her life, and it had ever since the house burned down. But that was almost over now.

There might be ten or fifteen bullets in the gun, but she only needed two. Kelly slipped around another log and moved into a small clearing lit by the full moon overhead. She tasted the cool air between clenched teeth and glanced up at the sky. It was black and empty, as though it reflected the void in her heart. When she looked back down, the breath caught in her throat, and she snatched the gun to eye level.

A child stood in the darkness on the far side of the clearing, sheltered by the shadows, little more than an outline against the night. Kelly wondered if she were hallucinating, imagining a physical reflection of the shadows in her mind, here to join the torment of her brutalized body with a vision of the child she never had. She ripped the hijab off her head, clearing her vision and exposing her face to the bite of the wind.

It wasn't a child. The figure stepped into the moonlight, and now Kelly could see the face in plain detail. A woman, barely five feet tall and as petite as she was short, with narrow shoulders clad in a tight leather jacket, and black jeans that clung to her skin like an exoskeleton. Two blades were strapped to the woman's hips, with their long handles glinting in the moonlight. Otherwise, no apparent weapons threatened Kelly's immediate advance. No guns. No other combatants.

*Was* it a vision? Some type of angel or spirit from Heaven, sent to hold her back from her murderous mission?

No. After everything that had happened, Kelly no longer believed in such things. If a person could walk, a person could bleed. She would make this woman bleed if necessary.

Once more, the woman stepped forward, and now Kelly could see her face in more detail. There were stunning green eyes and bright red hair, tied in a tight ponytail. She didn't look like a ghost; her smile, while sad, was too sincere. So genuine that Kelly hesitated, then lowered the gun a few inches in her shaking hand.

"Who the hell are you?" Kelly snapped. The words came out broken and disjointed, crowded down by the tears she struggled to restrain.

"I'm Lucy."

*Lucy . . .*

Kelly didn't know the name. Was this one of Reed's girlfriends? The bastard. So many women.

"Get out of my way," Kelly said.

Lucy tilted her head to one side. "Where are you going?" Her voice was calm and soft. In fact, it would have been soothing if Kelly was in any way capable of being soothed. But peace and reason were virtues now forever ripped from her life.

"That's none of your business!" Kelly snapped.

"Perhaps. I guess that depends on what you plan to do with that gun."

Kelly took a step forward. "Look, I don't have a problem with you. Don't give me one."

Lucy held up a hand, palm outward. "Listen, I think you should sit down for a minute, okay? Whatever is going on, we can talk about it. I don't want to hurt you."

Kelly's cheeks flushed red. Her entire upper torso began to shake as her shredded nerves gave in to the stress, and she swallowed back the bile that bubbled into her throat. "Don't you *dare* tell me what we can talk about!" Kelly took another step forward, shifting to the side to circumvent the smaller woman.

Lucy took a step sideways and laid her right hand on one of the swords. "I'm sorry. I can see that you're hurting, but I can't let you kill him."

Kelly's heart skipped. "*What did you say?*"

Lucy stared Kelly down without a hint of malice.

Kelly raised the gun. "*Move*."

Lucy shook her head ever so softly. "I'm sorry. I can't do that."

The pistol stopped, hovering over Lucy's chest, the muzzle a scarce twenty yards away from its target.

Kelly gritted her teeth, focusing in on the pistol's sights even as her hands continued to shake. "Fine. Go to Hell, bitch."

The gun cracked, spitting smoke and fire across the clearing. Kelly was vaguely aware of Lucy twitching—almost swaying to one side. As the air began to clear of the gunshot, Kelly saw that she had missed. Lucy, untouched, stood right where she had only a split second before. Kelly fired again. Once more, the tiny woman swayed to the side, then she took a step forward and slid the sword free of her belt.

# 31

**Winston County, Alabama**

Reed knelt in the middle of the cell and lifted the car off the floor. He trembled as he held it into the light, studying each tiny detail of the exquisite model. This was no cereal box toy—it was a work of art, with soft rubber tires and a fully finished interior. The headlights glowed in yellow plastic, and just behind the front fender, a silver monogram proudly declared the car's name: *Camaro.*

His gaze switched from the car back to the blood droplets on the floor. They came into focus now, beginning at the bedside and moving toward the door. Reed slid the car into his pocket and lifted the shotgun, his situational awareness returning as he followed the trail through the cell door and toward the end of the hall. The droplets led through another reinforced steel door, into a lobby, and then toward an open fire escape.

Reed lowered the shotgun, staring through the open metal gate. Outside, the haze gathered around the yard, sheltered from the blast of the overhead lights by the bulk of the psych ward. More drops of blood glistened on the grass, leading away from the building and toward a gaping hole in the fence.

In a moment, it all made sense. The fire alarm. The model car. Every unexpected circumstance of his attempted prison break. Reed's shoulders slumped as the reality of the situation sank in, diving through his psyche to that place where emotion met reason. He ducked his head and stepped through the fire escape, dropping two feet onto the soft dirt outside. The flashlight clipped to his belt clicked on under his now-steady hand, and he shined the beam through another hole in the fence, tracing the blood trail outside the prison and into the woods.

Straightening, Reed clicked the flashlight off, then slid it back into his pocket. He leaned the shotgun against the fence and pulled the burner out of his pocket. There was only one contact on the list. He punched in a short text message, then read it back to himself as he felt that old lump swell into his throat. He hit send, waited for the message to clear, then hurled the device over the fence and into the dark expanse of the woods. It crashed into the leaves a few dozen yards away, but Reed didn't wait to watch it fall. He drew the pistol from his belt, wrapped his finger around the trigger, and stepped through the hole.

---

The woods lay deathly still in contrast to the blaring sirens and shouts behind him. Each footfall crunched against wet leaves and dead sticks, and the fog that persisted around his shins made Reed think of old movies where the hero steps into some uncharted doom of forest or swamp, often never to return. He held the pistol in low-ready, one hand bracing the other as his index finger rested on the trigger. The darkness obscured his view of the blood, but it didn't matter. A clear path, marked by a random broken limb or disturbed pile of leaves, led away from the prison and into the blackness.

The yards slipped away beneath his feet like a silent river until the sirens were a muted memory, and the air around him felt thick and still. The darkness over his head blurred out the details of the path, but as his eyes adjusted, Reed could still see enough detail to remain confident that he was headed in the right direction. This path wasn't a secret. He was meant to find it. He was meant to follow it.

Ten more yards and the trees parted around a shallow depression. The dim light spilling through the trees was just sufficient enough to illuminate the forest floor. Drifts of undisturbed leaves blanketed the ground in a natural carpet laid by nature, and across the depression, there were no signs of broken twigs or marred dirt. The trail simply vanished as quickly as it had appeared.

Reed relaxed his finger off the trigger, then slowly lowered the gun. The stillness around him was no less complete than it had been three minutes prior, but it felt fake now, contrived, as though another being was there but suppressing their own presence.

"You should come out," Reed said. His voice was calm as he pointed the muzzle of the handgun at the ground, his finger remaining stiff next to the trigger guard.

The seconds dripped by, and then a footfall crunched from across the clearing. Reed resisted the urge to raise the handgun as a tall man appeared, dressed in a dark black coat. The man's face was obscured by a hood hanging over his forehead and casting a shadow over everything but his mouth. Nothing about his stance, his frame, or even his careful steps felt familiar.

"Good evening, Mr. Montgomery."

"Who are you?" Reed kept his tone low and calm, matching the other man's discipline and precision.

"You may call me Gambit. I work for a man who is interested in employing you."

"Why do I get the feeling I've worked for your employer before?" Reed demanded.

"Probably because my employer hired you to kill Mitchell Holiday."

An irresistible urge to raise the gun and blow this man into kingdom come flooded Reed's mind, but discipline overcame instinct, and he remained stock-still.

*Aiden Phillips.*

The name shot through Reed's mind like a bullet. Aiden was one of the last two surviving members of Omega Alpha Omega, the man Dick Carter described as a psychopath, a man with no remorse, no limits. Was he Gambit's employer? Reed decided not to tip his hand.

"If your boss hired me, he also set me up. He sent The Wolf and that fool from South America after me."

"The fog of war is a confusing thing, Reed. It causes people to make . . . regrettable choices."

Reed sneered. "Well, shit. When you put it that way, it just makes me feel all warm and fuzzy inside. I'm not working for you. I don't work for anyone. Not anymore."

"You haven't even heard my proposal."

"I don't need to. I know who you are. I know who you work for. Your boss killed Frank Morccelli. He killed Dick Carter, too. He practically killed Mitchell Holiday. And he *destroyed my father.*"

Gambit tilted his head. "You don't know, do you?"

Reed's brow wrinkled into a frown, and he started to raise the gun, but Gambit extended his palm in a calming motion.

"There's no need, Reed. Nobody destroyed your father. In fact, he's right here." Gambit snapped his fingers.

Sticks crunched under a heavy footfall, joined by those of a third person. Shadows moved behind Gambit, and then two figures appeared. One was a tall, broad man with thick shoulders and a powerful jaw, the kind of man who could've been an NFL linebacker. He maintained a dark glare beneath a bald head, and though he wasn't taller than Reed, his bulk was still impending.

The second figure was a thin man, clad in a white prison suit, his hair a mix of dirty blonde and grey, swept back over a strong forehead and a bold brow. A couple inches shorter than Reed, but with the same powerful frame, his shoulders were slumped forward in defeat, his gaze cast at the ground.

Reed swallowed, feeling a tear sting his eye. The gun trembled in his right hand, and he took a half step forward. "*Dad?*"

David Montgomery didn't look up. His face remained fixed on the ground, his jaw hanging half-open as a trail of drool slipped from the corner of his mouth.

New tears clouded Reed's vision, and he blinked them away. He raised the gun and glared at Gambit. "What have you done to him?"

The linebacker stepped forward and reached for the 1911 semi-automatic fixed at his side, but Gambit held out a hand, stopping him.

"Only what was best for him, Reed. Your father is a very brilliant man. A dangerously brilliant man. The kind that the world only sees once or twice in a century. You can't possibly understand what happens to a mind that powerful when emotions overrun it. Your father struggles from catastrophic anxiety. Unbelievable paranoia. His *friend*—my boss—has helped him into this facility to manage his—"

"Shut up!" Reed screamed. He fixed the muzzle on Gambit's chest. "I know what you did. You fried his brain! You fed him poison because he knew things Aiden couldn't afford to let escape. So Aiden destroyed him, the same way he destroyed Frank. The same way he destroyed Holiday!"

"Really, Reed? Is that what Carter told you?"

"Yes, dammit, that's what Carter told me. Right before your frazzled secretary minion shot him to death in his own office."

Gambit held up a hand. "Carter's dead? Reed, you can't possibly think I know anything about that. Carter was a friend of mine. A friend of Aiden's!"

"Sure he was. Just like Mitch, Frank, or *my father*!"

Gambit pushed the hood off his head, exposing a bold, handsome face crowned by black hair. He matched Reed's glare, then shook his head.

"Reed, you know nothing. Aiden isn't the villain here. I'm not the villain. And your father . . . is just fine."

Gambit turned toward David, his hand appearing from the depths of his jacket. A glistening needle hung from the end of a syringe, pinned between Gambit's fingers. Reed shouted and started forward, but he was too late, too far away to stop anything. The needle sank into David's neck, just above his collarbone, and Gambit depressed the syringe.

The world around Reed hung in deathly stillness as the seconds slowed to a crawl. David's eyes rolled back in his head, and he slumped, almost falling over. The linebacker grabbed David by the shoulders and suspended him in midair.

Gambit withdrew the needle and tossed it to the ground, leering over David, then he shot Reed a sad stare. "Reed, your father is here."

David twitched as the linebacker set him on the ground, his back against a tree as his hands lay limp at his sides. His head tilted back, and his eyes, once empty and full of darkness, glimmered. His head rocked back, and his jaw hung open. David faced the linebacker, and the big man knelt beside him, grabbed his head, and tilted it toward Reed.

"Look, Mr. Montgomery. What do you see?"

The world could've erupted into flames around him, and Reed would've never noticed. For a second, the fog consuming David's gaze parted, and Reed could see beyond—through the pain and exhaustion and years of abuse—into the soul of the weary prisoner. Into the soul of his father.

"Dad?"

David's lips parted in the faintest of smiles. "Reed . . . my son." The effort must have exhausted him. David let out a long sigh, then collapsed into unconsciousness.

Reed stood, his feet rooted to the ground, transfixed by the limp man in front of him. His mind exploded into a million confused thoughts and tangled emotions. Only years of ingrained discipline and practiced restraint kept him from hurling the gun to the ground and rushing forward. He had never wanted anything more.

Gambit rested a hand on David's shoulder, then turned toward Reed. His eyes were fogged with tears also, and he cleared his throat. "Your father is sick, Reed. He has an advanced form of mental illness that is destroying his ability to function under emotional stress. He is kept sedated at the prison, and Aiden—his *friend*—is expending every available resource to obtain his release. We never hurt him, and we have no intention of doing so."

Reed jabbed the muzzle of the pistol toward Gambit. "Give him to me and back off! I'm taking my father."

Gambit shook his head, the quiet confidence returning. "I'm afraid that can't happen, Reed. I want you to have him, but first, we need your help."

"I'm not helping you, asshole!"

"Oh, but you are. Aren't you tired, Reed? Aren't you exhausted of this cat-and-mouse game? You've been running for your life for weeks now. Oliver's men are on your heels. The FBI is breathing down your neck. Everything you loved and held is falling apart right in front of you. We don't want that. We never wanted it. It was a mistake to make you our enemy. I'm here to make things right."

Gambit took a couple steps forward, staring past Reed's gun as though it were nothing more than a laser pointer. "I know what you want, Reed. I know what your soul craves. Peace. Home. Family. The things this world has ripped from your grasp. Work for us, do this one job, and we will give it all back—your father, your freedom, your identity. One job. One kill. She's an unimportant person who's hurting millions of people—people my employer cares about. People my employer wants to protect."

Gambit held out an imploring hand toward him. "Don't be a killer, Reed. Be a hero. Do this job and walk away forever."

Reed's gaze switched from Gambit to the unconscious form of his father, then back. "Oliver made those promises. It didn't work out for either of us."

"I know. But I'm not Oliver, and neither is Aiden. Reed, so much in your life has gone to hell. This is your chance to take it back. And this man . . . *your father* . . . he's not gone. He just needs medicine and love, and you can bring him back. Please, Reed. Help me help you."

Reed watched as the linebacker cradled David like a baby. There was peace in David's expression. His chest rose and fell with the frailty of an eighty-year-old woman, but his heart was beating. There was still hope.

For a moment, Reed thought back to those distant memories of the pool, swimming with his father, laughing and loving, feeling alive and free. It was the last time he had a home, and every day of every year since had been spent trying to recreate those precious moments. Looking for a home in the Los Angeles gangs and then in the Marine Corps, then letting go of it all because he couldn't bear to see another person lose what he so longed to find for himself: A purpose. A belonging.

Every kill over the last three years, every silenced heartbeat, was one step closer to that invisible goal of finding that belonging—of finding that home. Maybe this was the moment he'd spent his entire life searching for.

Reed shoved the gun into the holster, locked his jaw, and faced Gambit. "I'll do it."

**SURVIVOR**
**THE REED MONTGOMERY SERIES Book 5**

**When bloodshed is the game, body count is the score.**

Elite assassin Reed Montgomery's private war with the criminal underworld is spilling across the country and leaving carnage in its wake. After identifying his enemy as a shadowy shot caller known only as Gambit, Reed is ready to end the war with a well-placed bullet.

But Gambit is one step ahead. After kidnapping Reed's father, Gambit proposes an exchange: He'll release David Montgomery if Reed completes one last kill.

The target? An innocent public servant.

With his father's life hanging in the balance, Reed must outmaneuver Gambit if he ever hopes to end this war. But Gambit is a master of manipulation, and he lives for the game.

The path to victory will drag Reed through a darker world than ever before.

# ACKNOWLEDGMENTS

As with all of my books, *Smoke and Mirrors* was the work of a village. I wish to offer special thanks to:

- My wife, Anna, who continues to support my work and the long hours it consumes. You are a true hero, and I love you dearly.

- Captains Shannon McCullar and Greg Stump, EDD, of the United States Coast Guard, who generously provided their time and expertise while I was researching Coast Guard operations for this book. I greatly appreciate your assistance with my work, not to mention the lifetimes of service you have rendered this great nation.

- My editor, Sarah Flores of Write Down the Line, LLC, who not only provided her usual excellent editing services but also served as my Spanish translator for this book. Thank you for your patience, because lord knows you've needed it.

# ABOUT THE AUTHOR

Logan Ryles was born in small town USA and knew from an early age he wanted to be a writer. After working as a pizza delivery driver, sawmill operator, and banker, he finally embraced the dream and has been writing ever since. With a passion for action-packed and mystery-laced stories, Logan's work has ranged from global-scale political thrillers to small town vigilante hero fiction.

Beyond writing, Logan enjoys saltwater fishing, road trips, sports, and fast cars. He lives with his wife and three fun-loving dogs in Alabama.

**Sign up for Logan Ryles's reader list at**
**severnriverbooks.com/authors/logan-ryles**

Printed in the United States
by Baker & Taylor Publisher Services